JESSIE HAAS

Keeping Barney

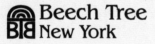 Beech Tree
New York

Published by Greenwillow Books
a division of William Morrow & Company, Inc.
1350 Avenue of the Americas
New York, New York 10019
www.williammorrow.com

Printed in the United States of America.

The Library of Congress has cataloged the Green-
willow Books edition of *Keeping Barney* as follows:
Haas, Jessie.
Keeping Barney.
Summary: Actually having a horse and taking care of
it, instead of just dreaming about it, turns out to be
more than Sarah bargained for.
ISBN 0-688-00859-3
[1. Horses—Fiction.   2. Responsibility—Fiction]
I. Title.   PZ7.H1129Ke   [Fic]   81-7029   AACR2

First Beech Tree Edition, 1998
ISBN 0-688-15859-5
10 9 8 7 6 5 4 3 2 1

For Scamper, with thanks

Contents

(1) The Dream

As soon as the sun gets below the branch with the birds' nests, I'll go in and ask them, Sarah decided. And this time I'll really *do* it. It was about the twentieth such decision she'd come to in the past hour.

The windows of the house stared at her like accusing eyes. She turned away from them, and wandered back through the barn. To her left, the empty haymow yawned darkly. Once it must have been heaped to the rafters with new-smelling hay; crossing her fingers, Sarah thought, Maybe it will be again, soon.

Before, the hay would have fed cows and huge, handsome draft horses. Their harnesses hung, cracked and dusty, on the wall, and in the back the handles of a plow reared up, skeletons from another time. What kind of horse would eat the hay *she* forked down into the

manger? Gillian and Albert said he was half Morgan, but
the other half might be anything.

She went down the stairs, pictures of what Barney
might be shifting through her head. In her favorite, he
was half Thoroughbred, tall, sleek and black, with only
the extra power of his frame to show that he wasn't
purebred. She leaned over the door of the stall that was
going to be—*might* be—his, imagining him there
within. At the sound of her voice his head came up, and
he trod, deliberate, powerful, and quick, to her. She
greeted him with the murmuring language that only the
two of them understood . . . and they whirled away
across the countryside, hurtling over walls and gates,
outracing even the deer . . . and the miles rolled away,
spurned under the hooves of the valiant steed, who
would race for her till his great heart burst. To calm
him, she leaned forward and put a hand on his hot neck,
saying only his name—

Barney. She didn't have the Black Stallion, she had
the *prospect, maybe,* of keeping a half-Morgan gelding
named Barney for the winter, and it was time that she
plucked up the courage to ask Mom and Dad. I'll just go
check the sun, she thought hopefully. Maybe there was
still a minute or two . . . but of course, the sun was well
below the branch with the nests, and she walked slowly
across the yard to the house, heart thumping.

Star barked when she came in, and Sarah hushed her
quickly. Mom was in the pantry, hunting for the bay
leaves. They'd moved here three weeks ago, and there

was still at least one essential thing missing at all times. Sarah didn't see what difference one little bay leaf could make to a Hungarian goulash, but Mom had high standards about her cooking. I suppose this isn't the time to ask, Sarah thought, seeing the irritated set of her lips.

The newspaper still lay on the table where she'd left it, open to the Classified Ads section. Wandering past it casually, Sarah saw her circled ad under Livestock, with a thud of the heart. It looked so obvious! Her face went hot, and she hurried upstairs to her own room, not wanting to be there when Mom finally noticed.

She got under the comforter to ward off the mid-September chill, and sat there, hugging her knees. Even through the bed she could feel the vibrations of Dad's typing in the room below. I hope *he's* happy, she thought, and immediately felt guilty at her own malice. All her life Dad had been writing, usually literary criticism, but finally, three years ago, his own long-planned novel. Incredibly, it had made money, and with it he and Mom had embarked on an old dream of theirs.

For the first time, Sarah learned that they owned a small farm in Vermont, left to Mom by her grandfather. When she demanded to know why they'd never told her, Mom seemed mildly shocked at her vehemence. "It was never a factor, dear. Your father's work was here, the farm had tenants, and that was that." But now, after giving suitable notice to Dad's college, the school where Mom taught, and the farm's tenants, they packed up their belongings and began the grand experiment. Dad was tired of sandwiching his writing in between everything else, Mom hated city life, and Sarah, more than anything else in the world, wanted a horse.

She gave the bed a discontented jounce. It wasn't fair. *Their* dreams had come true, why shouldn't hers? *I wouldn't forget to feed a horse,* she whispered to herself. Why couldn't they understand that? And *why* did they have to drag in all the undeniable financial reasons against having one? Now she couldn't even resent the decision without feeling childish and self-centered. *Nothing* was fair!

She rolled over and bit the pillow, trying to think of a good opening. *Would you let me have a horse if it didn't cost anything? Mom, what did you think of this ad? I know how I could get a horse for a while, just to keep and use. . . .* No, no, no. All those things sounded perfectly fine in her head, but she couldn't imagine actually saying them. She'd have to play things by ear, and she hated that. By the time she'd gathered her courage to say anything, the perfect moment had always just passed.

She heard the clinking of plates from the kitchen— Mom was setting the table. Already she knew the sound of the new routine, how many steps Mom always took around the table: had she paused by the newspaper? She'd definitely paused, but Sarah couldn't tell where. After a moment she moved on, once more to the stove, and then to the door of Dad's writing room. Then the call up the stairs: "Sarah, supper!"

Dad came out of the room as she reached the bottom of the stairs, looking tired and dissatisfied. Sarah's heart dropped. She followed him out to the kitchen, and heard Mom ask, "How is it going, George?"

"Slow." Dad groaned, sinking into his chair. "Have to fight for every word. . . ." He rubbed his hands over his face. "I expected this for the first few days, Helen, but it's been three weeks now!"

"You're pushing too hard," said Mom, filling his bowl with goulash. Star watched with bright, hopeful eyes.

"Don't encourage me to be lazy—it's fatal."

Mom gave him a very tender and exasperated look. "It wouldn't be *laziness* to just stop for a while and let your . . . your inner wells or whatever you call them refill. Don't be so hard-nosed. Slice of tomato, Sarah?"

Sarah nodded, tearing her eyes away from the folded newspaper by Mom's plate. She carefully salted and peppered her tomato and ate it in tiny wedges; the goulash looked unbearably thick and heavy.

The usual hungry silence reigned over the first part of the meal, but when Dad had helped himself to seconds, Mom said, "I take it you particularly wanted me to notice that ad, Sarah." Her voice was light, a lead-in rather than an accusation, but Sarah flushed hotly.

"What ad?" Dad asked.

"It's for . . . uh, here, it's circled."

Dad took the newspaper she pushed across the table, and read, frowning slightly. Sarah held her breath, the words repeating themselves in her head. "Wanted; someone to board one horse thru May. Hay and expenses provided, free use." She even knew the phone number by heart.

Dad looked across at her, the frown still between his eyes. Before he could say anything, Mom asked, "Do you know any more than what the ad says, Sarah?"

Sarah hurried into speech. "Yes, Gillian and Albert told me about him. He's a half-Morgan and his name's Barney, and he does everything—jumping and Western and driving and barrel-racing. Missy—that's his owner, she's away at college this winter—Missy's won *bushels* of ribbons on him." She paused, formulating her next sentence. "And there wouldn't be *any* expense, except maybe a little for fixing up the fence."

"I'll grant you that," said Dad, looking all too serious. "Financially it couldn't be better. But you know I had other reasons for saying no the last time we discussed this."

"But, *Dad,* I told you I wouldn't forget to feed a *horse!*" Star's long collie head lay across her leg, and Sarah stroked her remorsefully.

"Why not?" Dad asked. "And that's a serious question, I'm not just trying to hector you. I know you love your dog, I know you'd love a horse, and I don't see why there would be any difference in the amount of responsibility you'd take for their welfare."

"I think you're forgetting, George," Mom put in, "that to Sarah horses are such stuff as dreams are made on, and it's the dreaming that interferes with the responsibility. Having a horse around might just allow her to combine the two."

"What about in the dead of winter, when there's snow up to the horse's belly and she can't go riding?"

"Then there are dozens of other, *fascinating* things to do," said Mom, with a wry look at Sarah. "You can muck stalls and chip ice out of the water tank and sand paths and clean the stall out again. . . . But seriously, there's just so much more to do for a horse than for a dog . . ."

"And that's just the problem. I would seriously object if either of us had to do these fascinating chores, while Sarah curls up with *The Black Stallion*."

"But, Dad!" Sarah hesitated. This wasn't going to sound good, no matter how she put it. "I'd *want* to do all that. It's for a *horse,* and it's so much more interesting than just putting down a stupid can of dog food every night."

"And would brushing a horse be more interesting than combing a collie?" Dad's eyebrows gave a humorous quirk, but the words bit nevertheless.

Mom rescued them from painful silence. "Also, George, there would be more than you and I telling her what to do. There's all the horse books, which can be very stern masters, and there's also the horse's real owner. I think the experiment's worth making."

"An experiment with somebody *else*'s animal," Dad

growled, scowling at the table top.

Mom watched him a moment, and gently added, "And have you ever considered that having a horse might actually *develop* her sense of responsibility?"

"I guess I haven't," Dad said slowly. "But why should it, when having her own dog hasn't?"

"As I've been trying to explain, George, horses are different. Besides, Star is such a sweet scatterbrain, I don't think she could awaken many serious feelings in anybody."

Dad had to smile at that. "Here, Star," he called, and set down his bowl for her to lick. He sat there petting her, not saying anything, and Sarah gripped the edges of her chair.

Finally he looked up, his mouth relaxing in a rueful smile. "Well, go ahead and call them. We'll see what happens. I think the coffers can stand the expense of a little fence-mending." He stood up. "I'm going back to glare at my manuscript for a while."

Sarah slumped in her chair, staring glassily at his back. She couldn't believe it was all settled so quickly. Usually Dad was a lot harder to persuade than that. Mom was looking grave.

"He's very worried," she said slowly. "Do you understand, Sarah? He's faced with trying to make his dream into a reality, and it's not easy. I think you may find that out, when you actually have a horse. And now, why don't you call this number and see if he's still there?"

A new fear lurched up into Sarah's throat. Jill and Albert said that the O'Briens had been advertising for a long time, but somebody *had* to want Barney. She dialed—busy! Someone was on the phone right now, securing the right to have him. She let the receiver rest for forty seconds and dialed again, and again. On the fourth try, she got a ring, and an answer.

"He-hello, is this Mrs. O'Brien?"

"Yes."

"I'm Sarah Miles. I'm calling about your advertisement about the horse . . ."

Ten minutes later, dazed, she hung up the phone. Incredibly, the few people who had called about Barney had been "unsuitable," and Sarah had spent most of the time answering questions, about the barn, the pasture, and mostly about her own experience. Was three years of riding school going to be enough, she wondered. Anyhow, she had an appointment for tomorrow after school, to meet Barney and talk.

After drying the dishes for Mom and brushing her teeth, she went upstairs to bed, still in a daze. Nothing was settled yet, but everything was turned upside down.

She lay awake in the dark for a long time, scenarios of the future flashing through her head. She could hear Dad's slow, painful typing below. Poor Dad! It really was a gamble. They had the savings, and the money from the first novel, which to Sarah seemed like a fortune. Apparently it wasn't, though, and until Mom could find a teaching job they had to live as frugally as possible. Mom and Dad probably felt upside-down too.

But Barney wasn't going to be any burden at *all!* Sarah hugged herself in a sudden burst of joy, and tossed onto her side, trying to fall asleep so tomorrow would come faster.

(2) Barney

Mom met her at the bus stop, and twenty minutes and two wrong turns later, they approached the O'Briens' house. It sat, small, square, and neat, in the middle of a white-fenced yard. On the lawn was a tiny replica of the house, obviously meant for a cat. The barn was over the bank behind the house, down a narrow path that was almost a set of stairs.

Mrs. O'Brien came to the doorstep, leaning heavily on a metal crutch. "Hello." She nodded toward the path. "You see why I can't take care of him. Haven't been down there in two years, since my hip got bad. Going to have one of those plastic joints put in in January, but for this winter we need someone to keep him. My husband is a truck driver, you understand, and only home on weekends." She seemed eager to explain everything to them at once.

"Well," she said, after a little pause, "why don't you go down and meet the old boy? I'll put tea on, and when you come up we'll discuss this."

Sarah went to the head of the path and looked down. All she could see was the barn at the bottom, and a small corner of the pasture. She started down, turned to say something to Mom, and found herself off balance and running to keep from falling. At the bottom she slammed into the barn wall. She leaned against the rough boards a moment, nodding an answer to Mom's anxious question, and then pushed herself upright. Taking a deep breath, she walked around the corner, and there was Barney.

He was grazing in the middle of the field, a small, stocky, dark bay horse with a furry winter coat. When he saw them, he flung up his head and watched alertly for a moment. Sarah would have gone to him, but Mom, catching up, said, "Wait."

Barney dipped his nose and took an absentminded mouthful of grass, peeking coyly through his forelock. When they didn't move, he lifted his head to the level of his knees, and chewing, regarded them thoughtfully. Then he came over to them, his short, sturdy legs taking businesslike strides across the pasture.

Stopping before Sarah, he nosed her over with his squirmy upper lip, searching her pockets for treats. Sarah stretched out a tentative hand. Barney's strong yellow teeth clicked in the air an inch above her palm. Then his tongue wiped over it, searching. His ears began to droop disappointedly.

"Oh, Mom, I wish we'd remembered to bring him something!"

The absence of a treat seemed to have wounded Barney to the heart. He hung his head, eyes fixed on the ground. His bottom lip sagged, showing his teeth—a picture of deepest gloom. Sarah hugged his neck. "Barney, you poor, silly clown, you're not starving!"

"Hardly," said Mom, walking around him. "He's a butterball."

Barney certainly did present a rounded profile. He stood only fourteen hands high, broad-chested, round-rumped, and short-legged. His deep, shaggy winter hair made him look more like a Shetland pony than the sleek hunter Sarah had pictured, but he seemed robust and full of vitality.

Mom seemed to approve. She was walking around him, checking practical things like hooves and teeth. Sarah joined her, summoning all the knowledge gathered in years of reading the "Buying a Horse" chapters in her books. Of course, she wasn't *buying* Barney, but close enough.

"He's about fifteen, I'd guess," Mom was saying, "though frankly, the little I ever knew about aging horses by their teeth flies right out of my head when I'm confronted with the real thing. But he seems sound— you could swing baseball bats at those legs without hurting them, and he's certainly gentle."

"He's wonderful," Sarah breathed, gazing at Barney's mournful tricornered eyes. She stroked his muzzle, loving the velvety skin and the greedy lips that immediately searched her hand. Barney had texture, where her dream horses had only color and shape. "Mom, do you think she'll let us have him?"

"Yes, if she thinks we're competent to take care of him."

"But how do we prove that?" Sarah almost wailed. Now that she'd met Barney, the thought of not getting him was overwhelming.

"We've both got quite a bit of experience behind us, and I'm sure there's nothing to worry about," said Mom. "But why don't we go up and let her judge for herself? Come on!"

Mrs. O'Brien was waiting at the front door. She showed them into the living room, where a pot of tea under a pink cosy, a glass of milk, and a plate of cookies welcomed them. When they were comfortably settled, she lowered herself, with difficulty, into a reclining chair. A fat black cat peered cautiously out of the next room, then crossed to jump into her lap.

"Hi, Velvet dear," said Mrs. O'Brien, stroking the cat. "And how did you like the old boy?" she asked, when both their mouths were full.

Sarah washed down her cookie with a huge gulp of milk. "He's beautiful," she said thickly. Some crumbs lodged in her throat, and further words were lost in coughing. Mom took a ladylike sip of tea, and managed better.

"Yes, he seems to be quite a personality. By the way, how old is he? I couldn't quite tell."

"He's sixteen. We got him when Missy was eight and

he was six. Sal—no, *Sarah,* would you mind getting me that photo album from the television table?"

Sarah brought it, and Mrs. O'Brien folded back the cover lovingly. The first snapshot was centered in the page to show its importance. It showed Barney, a slimmer, sleeker Barney, with a pale-haired little girl on his back. A huge, supremely happy smile lit up the girl's face. "The day we gave him to her.

"And this was the day they won their first horse-show ribbon." The little girl, in patched breeches and a hard hat miles too big, grinned out at them. She held up a small, crumpled green ribbon that Barney was curiously nosing. Other pictures showed the little girl graduating to red and blue ribbons, to well-fitting apparel and a better seat; in a bathing suit, using Barney as a diving board; going to a Halloween party as the Headless Horseman; riding along back roads in the fall, with a background of bright leaves; a wonderful series of Barney rolling in the snow; spring pictures, with horse and rider mud-spattered; and one shot of Barney in an oversized work harness, plowing the garden. Sarah had to laugh at his dejected expression in that one.

The last picture was a fuzzy long-distance shot of Barney grazing. Missy sat forlornly on his back, her fingers twined in his mane. "That was the morning she left for school." Mrs. O'Brien's mouth drooped sadly. "She misses him so much. Us she can call on the phone, but not Barney." She stared at the picture for a moment. Sarah met Mom's eyes uneasily.

The picture seemed to call Mrs. O'Brien back to the present. She began asking questions: did they have a good barn, was there adequate pasture, how much experience did they have with horses? Sarah and Mom were able to satisfy her, and at last she said, "We *have* to farm him out this winter, but I can't do anything without Missy's say. If you can wait, I'll get her on the phone."

There was a long delay as she heaved herself out of the chair and crutched across the room, Velvet rubbing in affectionate hindrance around her legs. Then they had to wait for Missy to come to the phone. Sarah tried to stay outwardly calm, but her toes clenched inside her shoes.

"Hello, Missy? Yes, yes, how are you, sweetie? Yes, he's fine, fat and frisky as ever. Yes, Dad gives him carrots every Saturday. Velvet is fine, too—yes, she misses you. Missy—Missy love, quiet a minute and listen to me. I've got a little girl here"—Sarah's thirteen proud years winced—"who wants to take the old boy for the winter. I thought maybe you'd like to talk with her." She listened a minute, her eyes on Sarah. "OK, I'm putting her on."

Sarah stumbled across the room and gripped the receiver. "Hello?" She hated the questioning way she said it—that certainly wouldn't inspire confidence.

"Hi, I'm Missy. Mom didn't tell me your name." The voice sounded hurried and breathless.

"I'm Sarah."

"Hi, Sarah. I understand you want to take care of Barney this winter. Have you met him yet?"

"Yes."

"What'd you think?"

The question tumbled out so quickly, so proudly, that Sarah didn't have time to realize how important it might be. Her shyness vanished. "Oh, he's wonderful! He's so furry—just like a little bear."

"Bear is one of his nicknames," said Missy eagerly. "Actually, he answers to almost anything that begins with B. Even Benedict; I called him that the summer I was sixteen, 'cause I thought Barney was too plain. But Bear really fits him, especially in winter." A pause, perhaps as Missy realized that so far *she*'d done all the talking. "How much do you know about horses?"

Oh dear. "Well, I've had four years of riding lessons"—again, the questioning lift at the end of the sentence, when she should have sounded self-confident. "I've never really taken care of a horse, but I've read a lot." Looking nervously around the room, she spotted Mom, and added hastily, "And my mother had a horse when she was young."

The line was silent, while Missy thought it over. "Well, I've got to get him out of there. Mom worries—hmm. Well, just don't trust the books too much. Barney's read them all. Let's see . . . on the trail he likes to take shortcuts, so watch him. He has a ticklish spot over his right hip, but he'll only lift his foot when you brush it, never kick. And . . . darn, there's too much to tell over the phone. Give me your address and I'll write you a letter."

Sarah gave the new address, hoping she remembered it right. "Thanks," said Missy. "You'd better put Mom back on, then. Bye, and good luck."

Sarah held out the receiver to Mrs. O'Brien, looking dazedly at Mom. "She said yes."

"Wonderful!" Mom smiled, and her eyes narrowed in a friendly challenge. "Now go ahead and prove me right, girl!"

(3) Dramatic Entrance

Mr. O'Brien was to truck Barney over on Saturday, and Dad promised to help Sarah get the pasture fence repaired before then, providing that white-hot inspiration didn't strike. His grimace said *that* wasn't too likely.

The writing still wouldn't flow. At the supper table that night he sat silent, absorbed and angry. In the midst of her happiness, Sarah could sense his struggle, and unspoken fear. What if this had been a foolish move, as all their city friends had said? What if the dream wouldn't work? It meant as much to him as horses did to her. After a while, he got up heavily and went back to the writing room, and the vicious, sporadic pounding of the typewriter began again.

But joy didn't leave Sarah much room for worry. All winter Barney would be hers; her own horse, at last!

They would become friends. He would grow to love her, even more than Missy. He wouldn't want to go back, and in the end she would buy him. . . . She stayed awake for a long time that night.

On the bus the next morning, she plowed her way to the back to sit with Albert. It was weird to have her best friend on the bus be a boy, but Albert was fat and nice and read all the time, so none of the other kids paid much attention. He greeted her briefly, and buried his nose in his book again.

Sarah frowned. This wouldn't do at all. She was bursting with the wonderful news, but she didn't want to pour it forth to someone who was absorbed in something else.

"What're you reading, Albert?"

Albert started, blinked, and showed her the cover wordlessly. Science fiction, of course. Rockets and space suits—why didn't he read horse books instead?

"Is it good?"

"Mmm." Albert looked slightly distressed, torn between the necessity of making conversation and the desire to go on reading. Sarah knew the feeling, and she tried to catch him before he could escape again.

"Hey, Albert, guess what?"

"What?"

She exploded her bombshell. "We called about Barney yesterday and went to see him, and I can have him!"

A smile spread out from Albert's eyes. "That's *nice*," he said warmly.

"Nice! It's wonderful! It's the best thing that ever happened to me! My own horse to ride, all winter—I can go riding with you and Jill now, and we can . . ." Her voice trailed off. Between one moment and the next, Albert's face had iced over, and suddenly she didn't know what to say. The silence stretched on. With a distant, apologetic smile, Albert returned to his book, and Sarah just sat there, bewildered and deeply embarrassed.

Jill, however, greeted the news with an enthusiasm that made her red hair and braces glow. "Oh, Sarah, I'm so glad! I wanted to get him, like I told you, but Mom said we didn't have room enough with all the goats, and besides, all the other kids would be jealous and want to ride him. But if you've got him, we can all go riding together, if Alb will still let me ride Ginger. Oh, isn't it just *wonderful*?"

Jill couldn't have been happier, and gradually Sarah was able to forget Albert's reaction. But it was mystifying. Even Jill finally noticed.

"Hey, Alb, what's the matter? Don't you think it's wonderful? We've got all fall left to ride, the three of us, that is, if Ginger's still up to my weight, and then all spring—we can even go over Woodfield Mountain like we said we were going to."

"That'll be fun," said Albert, barely glancing up from his book. Jill made a face.

"Never mind him, all he wants to do is read. When are you bringing Barney home? I bet you can't wait. If it was

me, I wouldn't be able to sleep a wink all week. . . ."
Sarah never got a chance to answer half the questions,
but Jill didn't seem to notice.

Fence mending proved to be much harder than she'd
expected. The stiff barbed wire seemed to have a mind
of its own, and a very nasty mind at that. It scratched
and caught on clothes, and once, while Sarah was
holding it so Dad could hammer in the staple, a big coil
sprang away from her and barely missed his face. From
then on she gripped it as tightly as she could, but,
despite her care, they came in for supper every night
with new scratches.

Jill came after school Thursday to see the barn and
help with the fence, and on Friday they finished it.

"That should hold him," Dad said. "And maybe the
work has cleared my head; I think I've got an idea. Cross
your fingers for me after supper, Peanut." He seemed to
be right. That night, the typing sounds flowed evenly
and steadily, for a long time.

Saturday, Sarah awoke before her alarm clock went
off. She lay waiting for it to ring, and watching the gray
sky lighten to pastel blue. It seemed to take hours. The
house was completely still, save for the jingle of metal
tags as Star scratched an ear.

When the alarm finally went off, Sarah dressed,
tiptoed downstairs, and took Star outside. The barn drew
her, and she went to gaze into the stall that would be
Barney's. She could see him in it already, his eager head

looking over the door as he nickered a welcome. How long would it take before he knew her step, her whistle, how long before he came to love her?

After breakfast she sat out on the doorstep, to brush Star and listen for the truck. At every moment it seemed that it *must* be coming, but the wait was a long one. She kept going to look at the clock, to find that only ten or fifteen minutes had passed. Mom and Dad were busy and couldn't talk, and none of the familiar books could hold her interest, not even *The Black Stallion*. At twelve, she asked if she could call to find out what was taking so long.

"No, wait a while," Mom said. "It isn't polite to hurry people. What would you like for lunch?"

"I'm not hungry."

"You need something. I'll make you a sandwich. . . ." Star's triumphant yap heralded another vanquished squirrel. "Oh, hurry and shut her up. Your father's working."

Sarah captured Star and took her to the barn, avoiding both lunch and the clock. With nothing to measure it by, time seemed to move faster, but not fast enough. Finally, though, she heard the roar and rattle of a truck coming up the rough dirt road. She ran out to the yard as a short, smiling man got out of the cab.

"Hello, there, you must be Sarah."

"Yes, hello." What took you so long, she wanted to ask—but now that he was here the long wait didn't seem to matter much. Mom came out and said hello, and while Barney's hooves thudded impatiently on the floor of the truck, they discussed where to unload.

"Here's as good a place as any, I guess," said Mr. O'Brien. "Hope the little cuss'll cooperate. Took me an hour and a half to get him in this morning. Beats me— Missy just leads him, but I used up a whole loaf of bread teasing him up the ramp."

"He eats bread?"

"Eats most everything."

Barney turned his head anxiously as the ramp was lowered. Mr. O'Brien stepped up beside him and slapped his rump. "Get over, old man." Barney paid no attention. Mr. O'Brien squeezed past and untied the halter rope. "Back now, back. Stand away, ladies, he wants to rush."

Barney's hooves thundered briefly on the ramp, and then he was in the open, puzzled and snorty. He shied and blew at Star, then froze, staring at the barn and pasture. With his bright eyes and quick, nervous ears, he was a different horse than the one they'd seen Monday.

"He's full of ginger," said Mr. O'Brien tolerantly. He gave the lead rope to Sarah. "Here, you take him, and I'll bring out the gear."

She was holding Barney's lead rope for the first time. Barney, inspecting Mom as though he'd never seen anything like her, didn't seem to notice, but Sarah felt all the drama of the moment. The first time, the beginning . . . the bridle dropped out of Mr. O'Brien's arms with a jangle, and Barney leaped back. The rope slithered through Sarah's hand, and she clutched desperately at the end, just in time. Barney stared at the bridle in frozen horror, while she secured her grip on him.

"Come on, you've seen one of those before," Mr. O'Brien scolded. "I'll warn you, Sarah, he's an independent old cuss, and he'll get away with as much as he can. Isn't much harm in him, but don't let him out-bluff you." He set out a bucket filled with brushes, rags, and fly spray, and looked at his watch. "If I'm going to get some hay over here this afternoon, I'd better move along." He glanced at Barney, who was looking, bright-eyed, for something else to shy at. "Best put him in the pasture before I start the truck, or we'll be chasing him all over the next county. Want me to take him in, Sarah?"

Sarah shook her head. All the horse books said you should never let a horse know if you were scared of it, and the power in Barney's leap, his quickness, had made her as nervous as he was. "I'll do it."

Mom swung open the gate for her. It creaked on its hinges; Barney lunged sideways, jerking Sarah half off her feet, and jolted to a stiff-legged stop, snorting explosively.

"Barney," Mr. O'Brien warned. "Bring him up now."

Sarah tugged hesitantly on the halter. Barney ignored her. She pulled harder, and this time he took a reluctant half-step. They entered the barnyard that way: tug, step, tug, step, tug, step.

Once past the gate, Barney broke into a trot. Sarah

bobbed helplessly in his wake; she pulled as hard as she could, but her arms didn't have enough power to stop him.

"Step out to the side," Mom called. Almost by accident, Sarah obeyed. The change in the angle of the pull made it more effective, and Barney stopped. He dropped his head to sniff at a clod, and Sarah hastily unsnapped the rope.

"He'll settle down soon enough," said Mr. O'Brien, as she climbed the gate. The truck rattled down the road, Mom went inside, and she was alone with Barney.

(4) Bold Charger

They stared across the fence at each other. Barney looked even shaggier than he had Monday, his jaw bearded with thick hair and the outline of his ears blurred. He radiated robust health and spirits.

He blasted a snort at her and turned away, moving along the fence at a trot. His high head turned constantly as he neighed, loud and imperious. He must be looking for other horses, Sarah realized. His small, flinty hooves bounced him energetically over the barnyard. All that power; he must be just like Justin Morgan, able to do everything. She remembered the part in the Marguerite Henry book where the shaggy little plow horse defeated two fancy New York Thoroughbreds in two consecutive races. That was the kind of horse Barney was.

Getting no answer to his calls, Barney slowed inde-
cisively. The barn door stood open, and after a few
snorting false starts he plunged through. Sarah heard
the thud of his hooves on the boards, and then silence.

What was he doing in there? Could he get into the
spare stall? She couldn't remember if she'd shut the
door, but the barbed wire was in there, and a pail of
fencing staples. She hurried to check.

But halfway across the barnyard, she heard the rattle
of staples spilling across the floor, and the startled
thunder of Barney's hooves. He lunged, wild-eyed, out
the door, and raced around the yard. Sarah turned to
watch him, exhilarated by the sense of power in his
short stride. He was more showing off than scared,
shaking his head, flinging up his heels, skidding agilely
into the corners and speeding up along the straight-
away. "Faker," she shouted.

He slowed, and seemed to notice her for the first time.
His ears cocked speculatively. Then suddenly they
flattened. He squealed deep in his chest, almost a growl,
and charged straight at her.

Fear rooted Sarah to the spot, and Barney kept
coming. He loomed high and dark, and the drumming
of his hooves filled her ears. Right in front of her he
skidded to a stop, so close that the dirt spattered her
legs, and half reared, his head snakish and ugly. He
thudded back to earth with a grunt and a squeal, and
tore off across the barnyard.

Rousing out of her trance, Sarah whirled and raced

for the gate. Her body felt clumsy with fear, and the rumble of approaching hooves filled her ears. She clawed at the top bar and hauled herself up. Turning, she saw Barney just behind her, half rearing. Again, like a quarter horse, he spun on his heels and galloped around the yard, his neck bowed in an arch of triumph.

Sarah was still sitting on the gate when Mr. O'Brien returned with the hay. Barney had calmed down somewhat, but the sound of the truck sent him tearing around the yard again. "He's *full* of oats," said Mr. O'Brien, shaking his head in admiration.

He backed the truck into the upper part of the barn, and they unloaded the hay into the mow. Then he drove off with a cheery wave. Sarah climbed back on the gate.

According to the books, simply sitting there being human and alien should be enough to gain the wild stallion's interest and set you on the path to conquering his proud heart. But Barney seemed to be cast in a more self-centered mold. Instead of transfixing her for hours with an eagle's gaze, he roamed the barnyard for a while, sniffing things, and then began to eat.

Sarah watched awhile, gaining confidence as the calm stretched to half an hour. Mom came out once to look at him and, with a curious glance at Sarah's perch, asked how things were going. Not wanting to mention the charging, Sarah said, "Fine." This was something she'd have to work out on her own.

When Mom had gone again, she gathered her courage and slid down off the gate. "Hello, Barney." He cocked an ear at the sound of his name, but went on grazing. Sarah came forward, feeling bolder. "You're not really so mean, are you? You were just trying to scare me, right? You did a good job the first time, so don't try it again, OK?"

Barney raised his head slightly, still chewing. Sarah stopped, her heart in her mouth. But he only finished his mouthful and went back for more. Sarah edged nearer, close enough to touch his neck.

"Gosh, you're woolly! Got a coat like a bear." Barney's ears perked up. Bear was one of his nicknames, Sarah remembered. "Hello, Barney-Bear. We gonna be friends?" Barney snorted and shook his head—probably to dislodge a deerfly, but Sarah felt hurt.

"Yes, we are. I like you already, pretty boy. Won't you try to like me?" Maybe he's lonely for Missy, she thought. The horse of her dreams had never been pining for someone else. "You'll get to like me just as much, Barney," she whispered.

"Hi, Sarah, how's the charger?" Dad was standing at the gate, looking tousled and owlish after a long session of writing. Sarah smiled to herself. Charger indeed! "Fine, Dad. Come in and meet him."

Dad shook his head. "Can't. I'm still in my slippers. He settling in?"

"I guess so." She glanced doubtfully at Barney. Right now he seemed settled enough—the tricornered hazel eyes clear, the ears at a peaceful angle as he grazed. But she couldn't forget that fierce charge. She smoothed his mane nervously, and he gave her what seemed to be a scornful look.

"Guess I'll put the tack away," she said aloud as Dad turned to go. She ran across the barnyard, feeling a prickle between her shoulder blades. But when she looked back, Barney was still quietly grazing, ignoring her.

She arranged the tack in the spare stall until it looked pleasingly professional; brushes, fly-wipe, linament and saddle soap lined up in the feed box, saddle and bridle on pegs Dad had made, the leather darkly gleaming, the buckles shiny. Barney's bit was a thick, mild snaffle; chewed-up pieces of grass were glued onto it with dried saliva. Missy shouldn't let him eat in his bridle, thought Sarah, with guilty pleasure at finding a mistake. He must have a good mouth if he could be jumped in this mild a bit. . . . Suddenly, she wanted to ride him, and find out. She peeked out the door—he was cropping grass with calm intensity. He *looks* perfectly safe; why not?

Mom would probably rather she waited, but Mom was in the house, hopefully too busy to notice. Besides, she had to find out if Barney was going to be as awesome from the saddle as he was from the ground. Yes, she'd do it.

First, to catch him. He eyed her warily as she approached with the rope, but his evasive sidestep came a little too late. Once she'd caught him, he seemed to become resigned, and followed her quietly to a fence post to be tied.

He liked being groomed. Finding Sarah's first timid swipes with the brush not forceful enough, he leaned into them, grunting. Sarah felt a small inner glow. This was the first positive response he'd made to her. She made the brush strokes longer and stronger, enjoying them as much as Barney did.

She'd forgotten all about his ticklish place, and when he suddenly made an ill-tempered face and jerked his hind foot up, she jumped back. "What's wrong, feller? I thought . . . oh!" Missy'd said he wouldn't really kick. Mr. O'Brien had said, "Don't let him bluff you." Gritting her teeth, Sarah came close again. "Whoa!" Gingerly, she set the brush to the spot. Barney threw up his head, ears flattened, and menaced her with his hoof. Flinching in spite of herself, Sarah gave the spot a quick swipe and moved on.

He had a simple method to prevent her from picking out his hooves; he stood staring vacantly and pleasantly into space, and refused to pick them up. For long, frustrating minutes, Sarah pushed and hauled on his leg, to no avail. It was planted solidly as a telephone pole.

Finally, after she'd been tugging on his fetlock for a long time, he sighed and gave her the foot. It was round, cupped, and perfectly clean. Sarah stared in disgust at the remaining three. She was tempted to skip them; but no, that might lead to thrush. Grimly, she renewed the struggle.

When all his feet had finally been inspected, she brought out the saddle. Barney pricked his ears and sniffed it; thinking of Missy, thought Sarah. She settled it on his back, and reached under his belly for the girth. But the buckles reached only to the very tips of the billets.

"*Now* what?" She went to check the other side. No, it wasn't twisted, and it was already in the last hole. Back on the left, she noticed the black marks above the third set of holes. Apparently Missy had been able to girth him up that far once. "Boy, have *you* gotten fat! Be lucky if I can get it up to the first hole."

She did, but only after a long struggle and much heaving. Next, the bridle. Barney accepted it surprisingly well, opening his mouth when she held the bit to his lips, and not minding that she had to stuff his ears under the browband, instead of sliding them smoothly the way the horse-book diagrams showed. Encouraged, Sarah gathered up the reins and mounted. Barney stood still, ears pointed mildly forward. "C'mon, boy." She squeezed lightly with her calves, and Barney walked.

The first ride! This horse was almost hers, and this was their first ride. Sarah stood in the stirrups a moment, sinking her weight into her heels. In sneakers, she could feel his warmth and his long winter hair against her ankles. That was something new; she'd always ridden in boots. She noticed how little Barney's neck extended at the walk, compared to the riding school Thoroughbreds. His head stayed high, unrelaxed, but proud-looking.

"Trot!" He did, a little faster than she wanted. She'd have to slow him down, but first she wanted to catch the rhythm of posting to a short, quick Morgan stride rather than to a long Thoroughbred one. She kept getting behind and giving an extra little bump that shouldn't be there. Sitting to it was even worse. He bounced her high out of the saddle with each stride. As she tried to deepen her seat, to absorb the jolts in her body as she'd been taught, Barney leaned into the corner and the saddle slipped.

For a moment Sarah didn't understand. Suddenly, she was looking at the side of Barney's neck instead of the top, and the ground rushed by frighteningly close. She gasped and clutched at his neck. Barney abruptly halted, facing the fence, and Sarah managed to right herself on his back—except now she was sitting on the *side* of the saddle. Kicking her feet free of the stirrups, she slid down, and with a guilty start saw Mom crossing the barnyard. To Sarah's relief, she looked amused rather than disapproving.

"Saddle slip? Here, let me have a look." She loosened the girth, straightened the saddle on Barney's back, and refastened it. The buckle slid up easily to the third hole.

"How'd you do that? *I* couldn't get it that far."

Mom laughed. "Sarah, you've been had. It's called bloating; the horse fills his belly with air so you can't tighten the girth. Always walk slowly at first, both to warm him up and to give him a chance to let out the air so you can finish girthing. Now, hop up and let's see you two go."

With Mom watching, Barney was very good; a little fast, perhaps, and he did show a tendency to want to duck through the barn door, but Mom corrected that by standing there. Sarah still had trouble adjusting to his trot, but that wasn't his fault. His canter held a sense of power only tenuously controlled, but for the moment it *was* controlled, and the rocking rhythm was easy to sit to.

Mom said finally, "Well, supper's about ready. I think you'd better leave him in here for now, and we'll turn him out in the pasture tonight when he's calmer."

"What do you think of him?" Sarah asked, patting Barney's neck proudly.

"Well, Sarah, he seems very well behaved, and he's certainly pretty, but we hardly know him yet. It's a little early to be making up our minds, I think." But she gave Barney's neck a friendly pat anyway.

(5) Escape!

Pale but determined fall sunlight filtered through the filmy white curtains and slanted across Sarah's quilt. She lay sleepily enjoying it for a few minutes before she remembered—Barney! With a chill of delight she threw back the quilt and looked out, eager for that long-awaited sight; her own horse, grazing in her own field. The pasture seemed empty at first, and her gaze swept the row of trees along the edge. Still no Barney; but one corner of the pasture dipped below her sight—he might be there. Or he could be in the barnyard or in his stall.

Well, so much for thrilling first looks. Going out to find him would be almost as good. She slipped into jeans and a shirt and set out, carrying her sneakers to make less noise. In the kitchen, Star bounced around her, on the verge of barking. "Shhh!" Star yipped in reply.

Sarah grabbed her by the ruff and pulled her outdoors.

"All right, you can come, bad girl, but you have to behave. If you wake Dad up again . . ."

The ground was colder than she'd expected. She sat hurriedly on the frosty grass and put her sneakers on. Then she went to check the barn, though it didn't seem that a tough little character like Barney would spend the night inside. He hadn't, though by the looks of the bedding he'd explored a little.

"Come on, Star, he must be down in that corner." This was so much more complicated than just looking out her window. Still, it was fun walking in the chilly morning, with the frost soaking her sneakers and her dog at her side. With a quick shiver of eagerness, she came to the top of the little rise that hid the corner from view.

Barney was not there.

Desperately, she scanned the trees again. A dark horse might blend with the tree trunks, mightn't he? But she could see no movement. Good Lord, suppose he'd gone down to the road and gotten hit, or was caught in the wire somewhere? She whirled and bolted for the house. Star barked joyously beside her, thinking it all a glorious game.

"Mom, Dad, Barney's gone, I can't find him anywhere!"

Dad's tousled head poked blearily out of the blankets. Mom was awake more quickly, asking questions that were somehow steadying, even though Sarah didn't have the answers. "The gate was shut this morning? Have you checked your fence? Any breaks? If he got onto the dirt road, we have a chance of tracking him."

"I didn't really look. I'll go . . ."

"Wait a sec and I'll come with you." Dad was sitting up groggily, fishing for his pants.

"Pull yourself together and follow us when you can," Mom ordered. She pulled a pair of jeans over her nightgown and stuffed her feet into sneakers. "Let's go."

On the doorstep Mom paused, breathing the sharp air. Just knowing that she was relaxed enough to enjoy the morning somehow made Sarah feel less panicky.

"Did Barney have his halter on?" Sarah nodded. "Get his rope, then." She ran to the barn for it, and they set out.

The fence had seemed imposing and horse-proof when she and Dad had been repairing it. But Mom began to make annoyed little clicking noises as they walked along it. For the first time Sarah noticed the low wire, the weak splices, the huge gaps between one strand and the next. "I guess I should have checked this myself," Mom said, in a voice that despaired of ever seeing practical intelligence in her city-raised husband and daughter. But she didn't dwell on it.

They moved quickly along the fence, checking for broken wire and tracks. But they found no clues, except once a long strand of black hair caught on the top wire. That proved to be a false lead, however. In the bottom corner of the field they found where Barney had escaped. The badly spliced wire had given way—he'd probably leaned on it. Tracks on the other side marched purposefully down the hill.

"Do you think he might be going home?"

"Maybe," said Mom. "We'll follow to the end of our road and see which way he took. If it looks like that's where he's heading, we can get the car and drive over."

At the end of their road, though, Barney's tracks turned the wrong way, uphill. "Oh boy," Mom said, tucking her nightgown more securely into her pants. "Looks like we're in for a hike."

"But where could he have gone?" Sarah wailed. How was she going to call Missy O'Brien and say she'd lost Barney, on the very first night she had him?

"He's bound to be at the end of his tracks," said Mom dryly. They started up the road; Mom had an actual bounce to her step, and she looked excited. "You know, I haven't been horse-hunting like this in years. My old horse Mary used to escape every once in a while—I had to chase her five miles once before I caught her. But I always *did* catch her—a horse is a pretty big thing to hide. So stiff upper lip, hmm?" Sarah managed to smile in response. They trudged onward, getting colder and sniffly.

After a while, they heard a car coming up behind them. Mom looked down at the nightgown billowing over her jeans, and turned pink. Sarah turned to catch the driver's reaction, and saw their own car, with Dad at the wheel. Star pressed close to the windshield, barking enthusiastically as he pulled up beside them.

"Get in if you please, ladies." His voice held only a trace of its usual early morning burriness. "I've found your horse for you."

"What? Where is he?" Sarah struggled past Star into the car, while Dad watched smugly. *"Dad!"*

"He's at a farm about a mile up the road. A boy named—Alfred Jones, I think, called."

"Albert. Thank God!" Sarah collapsed against the seat.

"Oh, George," said Mom from the back. "You even thought to bring the saddle so she can ride back! This early in the morning—how alert of you, dear!"

They found Jones Dairy easily; a tall red barn, flanked at each end by metal silos and forming, with the house and outbuildings, a square opening toward the driveway, like a European courtyard. The pastures sloped down from the barn, and cows were already moving ponderously along the paths.

At the sound of their car, Albert appeared in the doorway, behind a wheelbarrow load of sawdust. "Be right with you," he called, wheeling it away. In a moment he returned. "C'mon, he's out back with Herk and Ginger."

Barney was grazing with Hercules, Albert's huge red gelding, and the Shetland Ginger in the middle of the field. The pony saw them first, and trotted to the fence, nickering greedily. Herky ambled after, poking his head over the fence for his treat.

But Barney, for once, wasn't tempted by food. He stayed in the middle of the pasture, cropping grass and watching them suspiciously. When Sarah called, he only twitched his ears in annoyance. Sarah glanced sidelong at Albert. He met her eyes, and smiled challengingly. Biting her lip, Sarah climbed through the fence, and with the rope hidden carefully behind her back, walked out toward Barney.

He wasn't fooled. He grazed on, watching until she was only a few feet away. Then he circled at a trot, pluming his tail and arching his neck. "Darn you!" Sarah followed, gritting her teeth. He circled again. Then, as she still pursued, he suddenly squealed, shook his head, and charged.

Sarah looked wildly for a fence, but none was close enough. She had followed him out to the very center of the field. In terror, she slashed with the lead rope. The heavy snap whistled through the air in front of Barney's nose. Then it whipped back around her, tangling her arm and slapping her side painfully. She struggled to free herself, sobbing in frustration.

But Barney, she suddenly realized, had stopped. He stood before her, snorting in surprise and dismay. For a moment she could only stare at him, shaken. Then she came out of her trance, grabbed his halter, and snapped on the rope. His ears drooped resignedly. He shook his head, this time a normal, domestic gesture, and followed her to the gate.

"You handled that well," said Mom, when she

reached them. Sarah flushed. She hadn't handled it at all; she hadn't lashed out with any real purpose. It had been only a panicked reflex. Albert's face still held the cool challenge.

Dad's frowning eyes were on Barney. "Helen, I don't care what agreement we made—if I see another display like that, he goes back tomorrow. She is not going to risk her life caring for a vicious animal."

"He was bluffing," said Mom quickly, "and Sarah showed him that she doesn't scare. Mary used to do that to me when I was small. Once I grew up enough to boss her around, she forgot about it."

Mom opened the gate for her, while Albert kept Herk and Ginger back. They tugged on their halters, wanting to follow their new friend. Serve him right if they pulled his arms off, Sarah thought darkly. She led Barney to the car and saddled him. This time, she remembered to walk him to let the air out of his belly. Then she mounted, sneaking a look at Albert to see if he noticed her professional ease and grace. He didn't seem impressed.

She settled into the saddle, and Barney turned to sniff her foot. Suddenly, she wished she had boots on. Sneakers didn't give enough support to her ankles, and they were thin if he decided to bite. Mom, Dad, and Albert were watching expectantly. With a nervous smile, she nudged Barney into a walk.

Barney didn't mind walking. The happy tilt of his ears

told her that. But he wanted to walk back to Herk and Ginger, who were calling him. Sarah hauled on the left rein until his chin was nearly resting on her foot. Barney continued to forge right, all the way around the barn.

Ginger and Herky greeted him eagerly, shoving their noses in his face. Three sets of ears jerked forward and back, nervously. Barney nipped at Ginger's nose; she squealed, and Herky drove her away, returning to exchange deep, wide-nostrilled sniffs with Barney.

All the while, Sarah had been kicking Barney's fat sides and heaving on the reins with all her strength. Except for an occasional flattened ear, her efforts went unnoticed. Ten minutes of useless struggle left her close to tears. She knew they were all watching, so she stared across the field until she thought she had her expression under control. Then she turned in the saddle to face them.

As she looked, Mom started toward her. Dad shook his head, looking a little worried but determined. Anger flooded her. Why *wouldn't* he let Mom help? All it would take was a hand on the bridle to lead Barney to the road. He probably thought that Mom was being too indulgent again, but . . . Then she looked at Albert and forgot her parents in hating him. He was enjoying this. He was smiling slightly, with his head turned so her parents couldn't see. Sarah's face flushed, and her forehead prickled with a sudden, angry sweat.

"Get me a stick!" Oh darn, *now* she had to start

crying! And he would know, from her high, broken voice. Well, she didn't care. Crying or not, she'd show him.

She snatched away the slim branch he brought, giving him a wet, vicious look that should have killed him. His face went blank with surprise, but traces of the smile remained on his mouth. I'll wipe that off! She slashed the branch down on Barney's rump, and as he leaped, she hauled on the left rein and screamed, "Now, get out of here!"

For a moment, Barney considered disobeying. But Sarah raised the stick again, and he turned sullenly away from the fence. Suddenly, he was extremely responsive, answering to the barest signal of rein and heels. Seeing this, Sarah had to bite her lip fiercely to keep back tears of remorse; but when he tried to turn around again, her anger welled up and she gave him another wack on the rump. After this he strode along like a trooper, angry, puzzled, but behaving.

Behind her, Albert called, "Hey, Sarah, wait a minute and I'll ride along with you." Something in his voice told her that her parents had asked him to. She ignored him, and in a few minutes they left Jones Dairy behind them.

(6) The Fall

Jill planned their first ride together for Wednesday, despite the discord between Sarah and Albert. They only spoke to one another when forced to, but Jill rose nobly above this snag in her plans. Sarah realized that she probably didn't notice anything wrong. Jill was used to other people not talking much when she was around.

Monday a letter came from Missy, full of what Barney liked and didn't like, full of concern for his well-being, and with almost no useful advice for handling him. After reading it, Sarah didn't even feel like riding; but if they were going out Wednesday, she'd better gain some semblance of control over him.

She rode inside the pasture that afternoon. Barney was on his best behavior, except when Sarah tried to slow him down or turn him somewhere he didn't want to go. All the books stressed light hands, and at riding school her own had been highly praised. But how *could* you have light hands on a hard-mouthed horse, she wondered, as the reins bit into her palms.

Tuesday she took him out on the logging trail that went over the hill behind their barn, to find out what embarrassing tricks he was likely to pull in front of Albert and Jill. Barney liked trails, and actually going somewhere, much better than endlessly circling a pasture. As he bounced along, full of interest, he responded lightly to her signals. Relieved, Sarah was able to enjoy the vision of a flaming autumn woodland, framed between two scimitar ears. This was the way she'd always imagined it, she thought dreamily, leaning forward to stroke the gleaming shoulder of her mount.

At that moment Barney decided to cut cross-country. He dodged into the brush, and a branch suddenly clawed Sarah's face. She threw up both hands to push it away, but it was too thick. Barney plowed on, and she was swept inexorably out of the saddle.

On the ground, shocked but not much damaged, she touched her scratched face tenderly. Ouch! She glared uphill at Barney, who had stopped to look back. He made a lovely sight poised there, all surprise and doe-eyed innocence, with his black mane and tail windblown and a big loop of rein draped over one shoulder.

"You *brat!*" Sarah scrambled to her feet and started toward him. He tossed his head, the sign that he was about to run. She stopped uncertainly. Oh dear, how could she keep from losing him in the woods, or getting Mom upset if he came home riderless? She had no food to entice him with, no way . . . oh, but wait a minute! There was a trick that had worked on Star once or twice.

Deliberately, she turned her back on him and started down the trail. "Bye, Barney. Have a nice night in the woods, with all the bears and porcupines. Serve you right if they eat you up." She listened—curiosity should be at work—ah, a rustle of leaves. She kept walking, and Barney's steps sounded behind her. In a few minutes he came close enough for her to turn casually and grab the reins, before he could realize he'd been tricked.

"There, gotcha!" Her face stung fiercely, and she had to fight down an unhorsemanly urge to give him a good hard swat. Instead, she made him stand downhill from her, where it was easier to mount. "Whoa, you! We're going a little farther, Mr. Barney Brat, and this time we're staying *on* the trail."

That night, soaking in the tub and reading—a book about a boy who tamed a wild stallion in one week— Sarah overheard her parents talking.

"Can't figure out where she got those scratches," Dad was saying. "She didn't want to say."

"I think Barney put her under a tree branch."

"What? Helen—"

Mom interrupted firmly. "I know what you're thinking, George, and he's not a monster. He's just a canny old fellow who knows how to get his own way."

"He picks some fairly dangerous methods."

"Any horse can be dangerous if your mind's not on him. Barney just bears a lot of watching. Besides, George, isn't this a novel role for you? Being overprotective?"

A silence. Then Dad's voice came, reflectively. "A difficult animal, eh? Well, as long as he's not terribly dangerous, I guess I'm glad. A bit of a tussle will do her good."

"It's from the difficult horses that you learn the most," said Mom.

Sarah rose resentfully from the tub, making sure they heard the splash. She knew exactly what they were talking about. Lately, Dad had become very worried over the possibility that they were being overindulgent with her; Mom agreed, but found it hard to break old habits, and Sarah found the whole affair very exasperating. The suspicion that they might be right only fed her anger. She painted her scratches with iodine—the sting suited her mood—and stomped up to bed.

Wednesday dawned clear, cold, and windy. Just the kind of day to put the ginger in a horse, Sarah thought apprehensively. Secretly, she'd been hoping for rain. All day she kept looking out the windows, but the weather stayed absolutely perfect.

After school, she hurried home to catch Barney. Jill and Albert were riding over to meet her—if *only* Barney would let himself be caught! The thought of them arriving to find her still chasing him around the field made her shudder, and shamelessly, she got a fat red apple from the cellar to tempt him with. Thus, he was caught, groomed, and saddled when Albert and Jill arrived.

Jill, despite her wiry build, looked huge on Ginger, she noticed. Herky's size balanced Albert's quite nicely. That must be why he bought him, Sarah thought maliciously. She swung onto Barney's back, aware that they looked just right together. With barely a nod, Albert headed around the barn toward the logging trail. Sarah fell in behind Jill and Ginger.

"Where are you kids headed?" Sarah turned to see Mom in the doorway, blocking Star with her legs.

"Just over the trail to Albert's." Star squirmed past Mom's legs and raced out, barking fiercely at the intruders. Barney shied, and Sarah, off balance, barely saved her seat. She felt herself flush as she caught Albert's sharp glance. "Let's go," she muttered, settling deeper into the saddle. Mom collared Star and led her back to the house, and they were off.

The first part of the trail led uphill, and Barney, with his energetic strides, began crowding Ginger's heels. Jill let them pass. But Herky was still in front, and that made Barney unhappy. His ears drooped in self-pity, and he worked so hard trying to pass that he had no time for mischief. Sarah had only to correct his tendency to try shortcuts. She relaxed, half-listening to Jill's chatter. There was a boy she liked who she thought *must* like her—he kept picking on her in math class, and . . .

Albert's back was straighter in the saddle than on the ground, and he seemed more self-assured and less fat. Sarah had to admit he rode better than she'd expected. Hercules, too, outshone her expectations. His long, clean stride ate the ground; Barney had to hustle to keep up, and they were always waiting for Jill and Ginger.

But going downhill wasn't as easy, Sarah discovered when they topped the ridge. The rocky trail hurt Herky's flat feet, and Barney, whose cuppy little hooves were like flint, forged ahead. In the lead, he was happy again. He also had time for misbehaving. He dawdled till Herky came up close behind him, and then bumped his rump threateningly. Sarah kicked him into greater speed, feeling hopelessly lacking in finesse.

Next, Barney discovered a rustle in the bushes. He stopped, legs braced, and blasted a snort at it. Sarah gripped him tightly, waiting for an explosion. He snorted again and tried to wheel, but for once she was prepared and held him straight. Frustrated, he backed up, his whole body expressing horror and shock as he stared at the rustling place. Sarah urged him with her legs, to no avail, and then tried slapping his rump. To do this she had to take a hand off the reins, and Barney promptly whirled. Now, though, Herky blocked the trail. Barney forgot his alarm in a nose-sniffing conversation with his friend, allowing Sarah to regain control. She didn't dare look at Albert.

They got straightened out and continued downhill. Barney shied at every noise, and Sarah had to keep a grim watch to keep him from crashing off into the woods. Her hands ached from clutching the reins, and she started at his every twitch.

At last they reached the end of the trail, undamaged save for Sarah's pride. A flat dirt road stretched before them. Albert glanced over at Sarah. "We always canter here. Want to?" Before she could answer, he urged Herky into a rumbling hand-gallop, and Barney was swept along by the other horse's speed.

He was in a racing mood. At Sarah's startled tug on his mouth he only galloped faster, flattening out to the road with mane streaming. Sarah tried to shorten the reins, but her hands tangled in his mane; she lost a stirrup; her hair whipped in her face and she couldn't see. She could only cling, and hope to ride out this pounding, jolting gallop. Dimly, she was aware that they had passed Herky.

Suddenly, the angle of Barney's shoulders beneath her changed. They were going downhill! Terrified, she hauled on the one free rein. Barney swerved, and with sickening clarity, Sarah felt herself leave the saddle. Her left leg brushed across the cantle; there was a terrifying mid-air moment, and then she was on her back in the road.

Her lungs were empty, she couldn't breathe. Desperately, she gulped at the air; alien-sounding grunts came out of her stomach, born of the struggle to breathe and the desire to cry. In panic, she clutched at the blur of color that was Jill, bending over her. At last, with one hoarse gasp, the air rushed back into her lungs. Slowly, with Jill's help, she sat up, wiping away her tears.

Albert rode up, leading Barney. His round face was pale and worried. "You OK, Sarah?" Sarah nodded. She didn't think she could get out even a squeak of a voice. The outlines of the world, even of Jill's close, anxious face, were blurry. She could only dimly see Barney, looking small and chastened beside Herky.

". . . way behind when it happened," Jill was saying, "but I saw it clear as day. You made a perfect half-circle in the air and you were up so *long*—it was funny, really, and I almost laughed, except you landed so hard. And then it was so scary to see you gasping and groaning— your face is kind of greenish—are you sure you're OK? You looked like you might have hit your head. Oh, Albert, suppose she's hurt her back! She shouldn't have moved. Sarah, lie down! Do you hurt anywhere?"

Nervously, expecting to discover a broken bone at any moment, Sarah stood up. Despite the wobbliness and blurry eyes, she felt most undramatically all right. But she didn't feel much like standing, she decided, and she did feel like throwing up. And her head was beginning to throb heavily. Her voice, when she managed to force it out, sounded furry and thick.

"Could . . . could you give me a leg up?"

Jill was behind her, holding her arm. "Are you sure you feel up to riding?"

Tears were starting again, hot against her stiff, chilled face. She giggled weakly. "No, but I don't want to walk either." She lurched closer to Barney, and Albert took her foot and eased her up. She flopped into the saddle; normally, Barney would have jiggled at this treatment, but now he stood quietly. Albert appeared atop Herky on one side of them, and Jill and Ginger flanked them on the other.

"Want me to lead him?" Albert asked.

"No." Scraps of memory—the horseman's dogma—always get right back on when you've been thrown. That didn't mean being led, it meant riding. Jill and Albert started slowly, keeping Barney tightly between them. He walked calmly now, subdued. Sarah braced her fists on his withers, still clutching the reins, and watched the brilliant autumn colors wash slowly by.

(7) Explanations

They halted in the farmyard, and Jill held Barney while Albert ran off to find his father. In a few minutes Mr. Jones came, lifted her out of the saddle, and carried her into the house. There she was bundled into a bed, while Mrs. Jones called Mom and Dad. They were over in minutes, and drove her to the nearest hospital.

The doctor, after examining her X rays and checking her sight and reflexes, said that she had a mild concussion, nothing to worry about. They should take her home and put her to bed, and no riding for a week. Hearing that, Sarah frowned. The doctor looked sharply at her. "And no nonsense about it, young lady."

He need not have worried. Sarah didn't want to do anything but sleep until the next afternoon. Then she awoke, to find her headache gone and her vision clear again. She was stiff and achy and very hungry; she hadn't eaten since lunch yesterday. Flexing as little as possible, she dressed, went downstairs, and fixed herself a tomato and mayonnaise sandwich. Dad was typing furiously in the back of the house, and Mom hadn't returned yet from a substitute teaching job. There was only Star for company. Sarah got the brush, and they both went in the living room and sat on the couch, Star's favorite forbidden luxury. For about half an hour they stayed there, Sarah lazily brushing and Star half asleep with pleasure.

Suddenly, Star sat up, ears cocked to listen. Then she catapulted off the couch and raced to the kitchen, barking. Sarah went to a window to see who was there.

Albert had brought Barney back. He sat on Herky in the driveway, holding both sets of reins—Barney looked as frisky and energetic as ever. Sarah hurried out, pushing Star back so she wouldn't bark at the horses. The cold gnawed at her feet as she hobbled across the yard, feeling like a rheumatic grandmother.

She held a hand out to Barney. He dipped his muzzle into it, scrubbing with his upper lip in search of a treat. Then he raised his head and blew thoughtfully into her face. She slipped her hands under his mane, to warm them and to scratch his neck. "What does that mean, feller? Sorry?"

"Probably not," said Albert, "but I am."

Sarah's head jerked up in surprise. Albert's eyes met hers, embarrassed but steady. "I was trying to give you trouble with him yesterday, and I guess I sort of caused your fall, cantering like that when I knew you didn't have him under control. I'm sorry."

Sarah frowned in puzzlement. She remembered the coldness yesterday, the air of challenge . . . but something like this? She looked at Barney's neck to avoid seeing Albert's painfully red face. He flung a rush of nervous words at her, trying to explain.

"It was because of Jill . . . well, that doesn't make much sense. But—y'see, Jill wanted to take Barney long before this and she couldn't. Then you show up and just *get* him. I know Jill didn't hold it against you, but it made me mad. Just didn't seem fair, and . . . well, it just made me mad, that's all. So I wanted to give you trouble. . . ."

Not knowing what to say, Sarah concentrated on the itchy spot under Barney's mane. As she scratched, he scratched Herky's side, and Herky, unable to reach anybody, wriggled his lip in the air. The embarrassed silence lengthened, and the cold penetrated Sarah's feet.

Albert must have seen her shifting them, because he said, "You should go inside. I'll turn him out for you."

"Thanks." With a last, lingering pat, she retreated to the doorstep to watch. Albert stripped off Barney's saddle and bridle and put them away, while Barney made a suspicious inspection tour, sniffing in the corners and finally rolling.

Albert came back to Herky, tied to one of the trees on

the lawn. Sarah, huddling her frozen feet, asked, "Um
. . . would you like to come in for some hot chocolate?"
She was too nervous and confused to make it sound as if
she meant it.

Albert said, "No. I guess I should get back for chores."

"Sarah!" Dad's voice exploded next to her ear. She
whirled to see him standing behind her in the doorway,
his hair all on end from the pangs of Art. "Get in here,"
he barked. "Trying to get double pneumonia on top of
everything else? Both of you, come in, warm up." He
disappeared again. Albert stared after him, his nice
smile beginning at the corners of his mouth. Sarah felt
suddenly more at ease.

"Come on in." This time it was a real invitation.

Dad was trying to find a pan for making hot chocolate,
but his mind was obviously still on his work. Sarah got it
out and made the chocolate herself. When Dad made it,
after a long day of writing, it either burned down or got
scummy.

That left him free to talk to Albert, and since they'd
only met yesterday, all they had in common was the
accident. Sarah hadn't had a chance to find out what
Dad thought about it—she'd been asleep most of the
time since it happened—and now she was shocked to
hear him say, "I'd like to ask your advice, Albert, if I
might. I don't know much about horses, but in view of
what happened yesterday, would you say that's a safe
animal?"

Sarah cast Albert an anguished look. He met it and

looked away, squaring his shoulder. "Well, that . . . yesterday was an accident, Mr. Miles. We were cantering and he got a little out of control, I guess, and then she pulled on one rein and he swerved—which he should have, he was obeying the signal, he thought— and she went off. He stopped a few strides up the road and let me catch him, easy as anything."

Over Dad's head, Sarah looked her thanks. "Hmm," said Dad, his face not giving anything away. Albert went on uneasily.

"Uh—he's not as steady as Herk, but he's a good horse."

"Ah." Made suspicious by his tone of voice, Sarah looked closely at Dad. He wore the faraway frown that meant his mind was on his writing. After a moment, nodding shortly, he rose and left them. Albert's grin appeared.

"He's a writer, isn't he?" Sarah nodded. Albert's eyes sparkled. With a quick, eager intake of breath, he started to say something, and thought better of it. Glancing uncomfortably at Sarah, he gulped at his hot chocolate.

"Um . . . well, you didn't miss any math homework. He didn't give any."

"Oh, that's good." Conversation died. They sat sipping their chocolate, growing more uneasy and incapable of speech with every moment. The silence became something almost solid, a curtain hung between them.

Star stood up under the table, rattling the mugs, gave

a sharp, bright bark, and ran to the door. Relieved at the distraction, Sarah went to the window. A battered station wagon was pulling into the yard, and Jill tumbled out the moment it stopped. She was talking before she got to the door.

"How are you feeling? You look lots better, but should you be out of bed yet? I made you some fudge this afternoon and Ma brought me over with it. It's chocolate with nuts and it needs to harden some more—except Ma thinks it might never harden at all. But you can eat it with a spoon, it *tastes* good. No, Star, you can't have any. Oh, hi, Alb! You bring Barney back? No, I can't stay, I gotta go home and milk the goats. Gotta hurry. I'll see you guys tomorrow." And she was gone.

Albert and Sarah smiled at each other dazedly. "Hi, Jill."

Albert looked at the clock now, and stood up reluctantly. "I have to get back for milking, too. Dad said I could be a little late, but he'll yell if I'm not home soon."

Sarah went with him to the door. "Thanks for bringing Barney back, and for telling Dad what happened."

Albert looked startled. "I didn't tell him *everything*."

"Oh, I don't mean *that*." Now that she thought about it, Albert's feeling seemed nobly loyal; she wasn't going to tell him that, but the episode was definitely behind them. "It's just—you never can tell what Dad's thinking, especially about horse things. I just hope he doesn't decide he has to send Barney back."

"Yeah, I hope so, too." Albert looked truly concerned.

"Barney's—well, lively, but he's an honest little guy."

"I know."

"Well, I'll be seeing you. Good luck!"

Mom came home a few minutes later. She and Dad started supper, Dad peeling carrots and telling her how the day's writing had gone. Sarah sat listening, wanting to be on hand when the subject of Barney was brought up. Besides, Dad's work was interesting. She couldn't understand why he couldn't just *make* everything come out the way he wanted. Whenever she asked, he talked about integrity or the constraints of reality, things she understood, but not in the context of writing stories. So now she just listened, waiting.

Mom put the dinner on the table—salad and a warmed-up casserole—now they were talking about how *her* day had gone. Weren't they *ever* going to talk about Barney?

Over dessert, Dad finally brought up the subject. "The Jones boy brought the horse back this afternoon." Sarah gripped the edge of her chair with nervous fingers. Things didn't look good, if Dad was calling Barney "the horse."

"That was nice of him," said Mom.

"Yes. He tells me the whole thing yesterday was an accident."

"Was it?" Mom turned to her. "You haven't really told us how it happened, Sarah."

Sarah explained. "Like Albert said, we were cantering and the road all of a sudden went downhill, and I tried to stop him, only one hand was tangled in his mane, so I just made him swerve." Best not to tell them that Barney hadn't been about to stop in any event. She remembered one more bit of favorable evidence. "Besides, Albert says he stopped right away."

"An admirable trait," said Mom. "My Mary always hightailed it home when she dumped me."

"Then, you still think he's safe for her," Dad said, frowning.

"No horse is completely safe, George. They're timid, and their instincts all tell them to flee if there's any doubt at all of their safety. Besides that, they can be God-awfully set in their ways. Still, for so powerful an animal, they're amazingly gentle."

"But they *can* be vicious, anything can be vicious, and I want to know if Barney is. Specifics, not generalities, Helen."

Instead of answering, Mom turned to Sarah. The look forced her to be honest. "Well, he's pretty hard to handle sometimes—he never lets me forget he's older than me—but he's pretty trustworthy, too. He—I don't know if I *could* have stopped him yesterday, but he definitely didn't mean to throw me. He looked as shocked as I was."

Mom gave her an appreciative smile. "I thought that might have been the case. No, George, I don't think you have to worry too much about Barney."

"I'll have to take your word for it," said Dad, though it seemed that he entertained a few lingering doubts.

(8) A Letter

So Barney stayed. By Friday Sarah could go out to groom him, though she wasn't allowed to even think of getting on. She went eagerly to the barnyard, hoping for a nicker, signs of friendship and being missed. Barney nuzzled her, found the apple core she'd brought, and went back to grazing. He wants Missy, of course, Sarah thought. But she's not here, and maybe she'll fall in love. College kids always do that . . . and then she won't want you anymore, and I can buy you. Feeding herself on dreams, she could ignore his indifference.

On Wednesday she was in the saddle again. To be on the safe side, she rode only around the field that first day. Barney behaved about as well as usual; that is, he always went a little faster than Sarah wanted, and unless she was strong-armed enough to pull him back on course, he went where he wished. Time after time Sarah came out of a daydream to find herself somewhere she'd had no intention of going, Barney having refused the role of obedient, mind-reading steed.

Her afternoons settled into a satisfying pattern; she checked the mailbox and walked up the road, had a snack, changed her clothes and went riding, sometimes with Albert and Jill, sometimes just with Albert, sometimes alone. She would come home to find supper cooking. After dinner came homework, a bath, and a long read in bed before turning out the light.

Then, one cold day in late October, she opened the mailbox to find a letter from Missy.

Dear Sarah,

Hi. How's my Barney Bear doing? Just thought I'd write to tell you I'll be back for a week over Thanksgiving, and will be taking him home with me.

Have there been any problems? I expect so. Barney can be a monster in the fall. Remember, be firm with him, but go easy on his mouth. I don't want it ruined. Not that I mean to suggest you would, but it would be easy to be too firm with him, in some of the moods he gets into. And if you haven't started him on hay yet, he should be getting some now, about three-quarters of a bail per day. Sprinkle it with water if it's at all dusty—can't take a chance of him getting heaves.

Well, I'll sign off now. Say hi to him for me, and
tell him I'll be seeing him soon.

Yours truly,
Missy

Sarah's heart sank. Slowly she folded the letter and
put it in her schoolbag. Of course Missy would want
Barney on vacations. She'd never thought of that.

Had she been doing things right? "Go easy on his
mouth." Uncomfortably, she remembered all the times,
yesterday alone, that she'd hauled on the reins to stop or
slow or turn him. Good lord, suppose she'd ruined him!
But what else could she do? He wouldn't do *anything*
unless she pulled him. Turning her hands over, she
examined the callouses the reins had made. *Callouses!*
Her hands had been the lightest of all her class at riding
school. And remembering the long, bland faces of the
horses she'd ridden there, she groaned. How could *they*
teach her anything about how to handle Barney?

She scuffed somberly home through the brown
leaves. Star greeted her at the door, but Sarah pushed
her aside absently and went into the kitchen. She got an
apple for a snack. Instead of rushing out to Barney the
way she usually did, she paused to read the funnies in
the paper. She didn't feel like facing Barney so soon
after being reminded that he wasn't hers. If she hadn't

promised to meet Albert, she wouldn't have gone riding at all.

Albert, looking like a plump apple in his red winter coat, met them halfway to Jones Dairy. "Hi, Sarah," he sniffled. Cold had turned his nose as red as the coat. "You want to go on the trail by Bemis's camp? We're kind of late, and that's short enough to get me back in time for chores. 'Sides, it gets dark early now, without daylight savings."

Sarah groaned, sympathizing with the disgust in his voice. The time change cut them short an hour of riding time.

A few feet farther they turned off the road, up a steep, shale-covered trail. Albert took the lead so they could talk. If Sarah turned her attention backward, Barney would immediately think up some naughtiness and do it. But today, she didn't feel like talking, and after two attempts to start a conversation, Albert left her to her own gloomy thoughts.

Barney was beginning to blow at the steepness of the hill, sending clouds of steamy breath up around his head. Sarah loosened the reins and leaned forward in the saddle, taking her weight off his hindquarters.

They heaved up to level ground at last, and before Sarah could tighten the reins, Barney ducked into the brush. For a moment they crashed along, Sarah helpless to stop him. Then a branch caught one of her braids, hauling her backward; it felt like it was ripping out of her head. *"Whoa,"* she shrieked. Barney stopped, but only because he'd gotten his feet tangled in some saplings. He tossed his head fretfully. Hearing nothing from Albert, Sarah rolled an eye backward. He was continuing up the trail, serenely unaware.

"Bert!"

"Yeah?" He turned in the saddle, and gave a shout of laughter.

"Hey, it's not funny! Come get us loose!"

"It is *so* funny! You should see yourself—you look like you're taking a nap on him, with an invisible pillow Wish I had a camera."

"He's pulling my hair out," Sarah shrieked. "Hurry *up*, will you?"

"Hold on a sec," said Albert, still snickering. She heard him dismount, and a rustle as he tied Herky to a branch. "Whoa, Barney." He was beside her. "Darn, I can't reach your hair to untangle it. Can you get it if I hold him still?"

"Um . . ." She felt out along the braid with one hand. "I guess so." She dropped the reins. Albert's "Wait!" came simultaneously with Barney's worried fidget. Air beneath her, a wrench at her braid, and she was flat on the ground, looking up at Barney's stomach and Albert's grin.

"All right?"

"Ouch!" She got up, rubbing her head. "Lucky I've got any hair left. Ow!"

Albert patted Barney's neck.

"He's a good old guy, Sarah. He could have kicked your brains out when you fell; a lot of horses would have."

"Oh, he's a great old guy. He'll only *half* kill you. How are we going to get him loose?"

"Let him alone, and he'll figure it out himself."

Given his head, Barney sniffed the tangle around his feet. Then, steadily and carefully, he picked his way backward. Free, he shook himself till the saddle creaked, and trotted over to tell his troubles to Herky. Sarah caught him and mounted, praising him for being so clever—which was ridiculous, since the whole thing was his own fault, but he *had* been smart and sure-footed.

"Gotta hurry," said Albert, putting Herky into a trot. "Can't be late for chores."

Posting quickly to the gay jounce of Barney's trot, Sarah called, "Why not? It's only your father—he wouldn't fire you."

"Yeah, but we run on the cows' schedule, not the people's. They have to be milked at the same time every day or production falls off. Gotta get 'em in at five-thirty, then I feed 'em and the calves, and help finish up the milking."

"When do you get any time for yourself?" Sarah asked, thinking of her own self-indulgent schedule.

Albert sighed sharply. "There isn't much. I have to do

homework right after supper, and if I want to do any
writing, I have to do it after Mom thinks I've gone to
bed."

"You write stories?"

Albert's ears flamed. "Yeah, some."

That explained his interest in Dad. "What kind of
stories do you write?"

"Science fiction," Albert mumbled, closing his legs
tighter on Herky's sides. The big red gelding lengthened
his stride, and Sarah decided not to pry. He probably
thought writing was unmanly or something stupid like
that, but anyway, she wouldn't press him.

They started downhill. Sarah's cold hands were stiff
on the reins, and her nose felt a little drippy. Her ankles
were tired, too. But the world looked incomparably
better from fourteen hands up, framed between an alert
pair of ears. She wiped her nose on her jacket sleeve and
hummed the part of "The Happy Wanderer" that she
could remember.

The trail came out behind the Joneses' cornfield. A
long tractor road led straight through the middle of the
field, perfect for cantering. Herky had to walk now, to
come in cool, but Sarah could take advantage of the
opportunity. She trotted up to come even with Albert.

"See you at the barnyard."

Barney jiggled, and she gave him his head. His canter
was bouncy, but the bounciness and his long, flying
mane gave a sense of great speed. He had a fiery way of

snorting every few strides and striking out harder than usual with one front foot. The tempo of hoofbeats exhilarated her. They were running the Kentucky Derby—no, they were Secretariat and Ron Turcotte in the Belmont, and Herky was the vanquished field, thirty-one lengths back. No, they were in the pony express, being chased by—

Suddenly they were at the end of the cornfield, thundering up the lane that ran between two pastures to the barn. Startled at being there so soon, Sarah tried to stop Barney. And tried harder. Barney's neck bowed until his chin touched his chest, but he plowed on. Desperately, Sarah hauled on the reins. He'd run into the barn, or worse, he'd turn too quickly. . . .

A sharp, silvery neigh pierced the wall of wind around her head. She caught a glimpse of flying mane as Ginger raced to the fence to meet them. Barney, neck still bowed iron-hard, pricked his ears toward her. He's going to swerve! She abandoned the reins and grabbed his mane, just in time. He ducked toward the fence and stopped, in two bounces. Only her hold on his mane kept Sarah from flying forward onto the barbed wire.

She was still sitting there, shaken, when Albert rode up. "Boy, Sarah, you're the only person I know who doesn't even realize when she's being run away with! You didn't even *try* to stop him."

Sarah nodded wearily. "I know." With difficulty, she pulled Barney away from the fence, and they continued up the lane. "See you tomorrow," Sarah said when they got to the yard, and rode down the road.

Fool! Daydreaming while Barney ran away! If he'd dumped her onto that fence, Dad would have sent him back for sure. Why couldn't the little creep be good? And where was the rapport you were supposed to develop with your mount, the respectful give and take, the responsiveness and trust?

Missy'll have you back soon enough, she thought morosely. Obviously you belong together. . . . Sunk in the gloom of this thought, she rode slowly home.

(9) Missy

Sarah peeled the last sliver of red skin from the last naked white apple, split it, and cut the core into the pan of parings. There, *that* was done. She got her coat and went to take the cores out to Barney.

He was eating hay in a corner of the huge box stall, but he turned eagerly when she came in, and nickered. It was more in greed than friendship, since he'd been reaping the benefits of Thanksgiving cooking all week long. Still, it was a homey, comfortable sound. Sarah emptied the pan into the oak feed box, and he nudged her aside. She watched him slobber and fumble, his busy tongue and lips searching the corners to make sure he'd gotten it all. "Pig." She ran her fingers through his deep coat. He felt warm; he smelled warm, too, as she pressed her face against his shoulder, warm and dusty and pungently horsey. Was there time for a ride?

She went to the door to look at the sky. It hung low-bellied and sullen, threatening snow. Dad's parents were driving up tonight from Boston for Thanksgiving. She hoped the snow would hold off till they arrived. Gramp regarded bad weather as a personal challenge from Nature, and never deigned to adjust his schedule to it.

She went in to check the time—only two. "Mom, I'm riding," she called.

"OK, dear, but I need help with the pies in a while."

"All right," Sarah groaned. She hated making pie. It was hard to get right, and she always spilled flour all over everything. But Mom, who was also an only child, had always made the Thanksgiving pie with *her* mother, and that's the way it had to be. Sarah had to admit, when they were set out on the table, that they were worth the work.

She led Barney outside and tacked up, remembering to warm the bit with her breath as the cowboy hero always did. Her bulky winter coat made mounting harder, and already her fingers were red and stiff. She needed gloves; mittens were no good for riding. Maybe for Christmas . . .

Riding in the pasture wasn't as unvaried as it sounded; Barney did his best to make it interesting. On the flat at the bottom, he turned and stopped like a dressage champion, at the lightest pressure, and Sarah dreamed dreams of three-day event triumphs. But going uphill toward the barn he shattered them, going like a freight train with the brakes gone. There were a dozen degrees in between, depending on whether he was watching something, or feeling good, bored, or spooky. Was his mouth soft or hard? Iron gloved in velvet, Sarah decided. Which meant, really, that he did what he pleased.

They were on the flat now, and she tried a canter, a short one because of the frozen ground. Barney stepped into it willingly, but without his usual explosion. She pulled him in after a few strides; two trotting steps, two walking steps, and a smooth, square halt. "Barney, I just don't understand you!"

Barney tossed his mane arrogantly. Of course she didn't. He wasn't meant to be understood. He thrust his nose down, pulling Sarah forward onto his neck, and snatched a mouthful of brown grass. Sarah pulled him up. "No, Barney! That's a bad habit, and I don't *care* if Missy let you. While you're my horse, you don't." And you're not my horse for long, now. Wonder why she hasn't come yet?

To quell these thoughts, she put Barney into a working trot, and worked for a while on keeping her legs steady while she posted. But she couldn't concentrate— her mind kept jumping to Missy and how much better *she* probably did it.

At last, with a sigh, she let Barney walk. "OK, we'll go back along the fence line now, and see if we can see a deer."

The chances weren't too good, now that it was hunting season, but there was another reason. Going along the fence, they got quite close to the barn before they could see it, as it was hidden behind the hill. That meant a shorter distance in which to fight the losing battle to slow Barney down.

As she'd expected, they saw only squirrels and blue jays. She'd fallen in love with the jays, so beautiful and smart and bad-mannered. "Just like you, Bear." Barney dipped his muzzle innocently. Then his ears swept forward as the barn came into sight, the barn which promised hay, unsaddling, and rest. Sarah snatched up a length of rein, but too late to keep him from breaking into a canter. His neck bowed like a war-horse, he strode on. Sarah was still hauling futilely on the reins when they swept through the gate. Barney skidded to a halt at his usual fence post, and tossed his head triumphantly. He'd won again.

Suddenly, a thin, trilling whistle cut the air. Barney swung his head around, his ears straining forward. Sarah turned, too, and saw a small, pale-haired girl running toward them. A loud nicker burst from Barney's throat, far different from the greedy little sound he made for Sarah. The girl flung her arms around his neck, while Sarah sat frozen in the saddle.

They stood that way awhile, Missy's face buried in Barney's mane, his nose scrubbing her back pocket. Then Missy stepped back and looked at his head, stroking the flat of the cheek and the hollows above his eyes, fluffing his forelock. All the while she talked to him, in a barely audible voice.

It was like watching two people kiss in a bus station. Sarah dismounted to go, then stopped, paralyzed, as Missy's hand found one of the raw patches by Barney's mouth, where the bit rubbed when he pulled too hard.

She closed one hand over his nose and turned his head firmly so she could see. The little patch showed up terribly red to Sarah's frightened eyes. The color rose in Missy's face, but she only folded her lips tightly and turned away. When she looked at Sarah again, she showed no expression. "Hello, are you Sarah?"

"Yes," Sarah gulped.

"I'm Missy. I've come to take Barney home for a while, as I wrote you I would. He . . . he looks to be in good shape."

Sarah's face went hot. "Those sores . . . I'm . . . I put Vaseline on. . . ."

Missy touched the raw patch tenderly. "Yes, Vaseline's the thing to use. But you shouldn't . . ." She stopped abruptly, folding her lips again.

"I *know* he shouldn't have them at *all*, but he pulls so and I have to pull too or I can't make him do anything." She broke off, hating the wail in her voice. Missy ducked her head and pinched the bridge of her nose.

"I realize it's difficult," she said finally, and Sarah could hear the barely controlled tremble in her voice. "But you *can't* . . . no, not now!" Very flushed, she shook her head and turned away. "I . . . I have to get home quickly, before it starts snowing. Will you please—there's a grain bag in the doorway of the barn. Will you please put the brushes and hoofpick and . . . the Vaseline . . . in for me? Thank you."

Sarah got the things, trembling inwardly, and gave the bag to Missy, already on Barney's back, straight and terrible and angry as Joan of Arc on her charger.

"Thanks," she said again, and whirling Barney with barely a touch of the reins, she rode away. Stunned, Sarah watched them go down the driveway, Missy riding slim and easy on a loose rein, and the first snowflake caught in Barney's black tail.

(10) Thanksgiving

Sarah lay on her bed, listening to the sounds from downstairs—clinks and clatters as Dad and Gramp did the Thanksgiving dishes, their voices, music on the stereo. She should be down there being sociable, but it was impossible. Gramp kept saying she should stop moping, look alive, take an interest in something, and Gram was always asking questions about "her" horse. Barney was the last thing she wanted to talk about right now.

She rolled over, staring at the row of books along the opposite wall. She knew exactly which pleasures each held, and none was quite what she wanted. Restlessly, her gaze wandered around the room, lighting finally on the one picture she had of Barney. Mom had taken it as they came into the yard after that horrible morning at

Albert's. Her tears had dried, and Barney looked pretty, cheerful, and virtuous. It reminded her of the pictures at Missy's house. From that, she looked to her old riding school ribbons, hung above her bureau. They conjured up a picture of long-faced, docile horses endlessly circling a ring.

All her old pride of accomplishment was gone. After all, what was so great about being able to sit in perfect form, with light hands, on smooth-gaited, mild-mannered Thistledown? If he'd ever had an independent thought in his life, it must have been back before he was weaned. He was lovely, amiable, tractable, and competent—but he never *did* anything.

If I could learn to ride *Barney,* it'd really mean something, she thought. If he ever responded the way Thistledown had, it would mean that she'd gained his love, that he was really *her* horse . . . but how could that ever happen? Even if Missy *did* bring him back. . . .

There was a knock, and Mom looked around the door. "Sarah?"

"Yes. What, Mom?"

"Just seeing what you're up to." She crossed over to the bed and sank down, sighing. "Oh, I'm getting old. Thanksgiving preparations tire me more than an all-day ride used to." She leaned back, eyes closed. After a few minutes, when neither of them had spoken, she said quietly, "Something more is bothering you than just losing Barney for a week, isn't it?"

Sarah didn't answer for a while. Somehow it seemed hard to lead directly into the subject. Finally, she asked, "Was your Mary hard to handle?"

"She was an old darling," said Mom. "She just knew how to get her own way. At first she only did what *she* wanted, and when I scolded, she'd give me this big-eyed, hurt look as if to say, 'But I didn't understand!' And she had countless tricks—shying, pretending to stare at something faraway, acting lame or sick or sad or bored—she was a wise old mare. I ended up being able to outfox her most of the time, but we were never completely sure which one of us ran the show." Sarah could look up now. Mom's eyes were faraway, resting affectionately on an old white mare.

"Do you miss her?"

"No, dear," said Mom slowly. "It's been many years now, and I've gotten used to living without her. But I loved her very much. She was a good friend."

"A friend, when she did all that?" Sarah was thinking of Barney's tricks and stubbornness that made her despair of ever establishing the proper horse-rider relationship.

"Oh sure, hon. It's just the way they are. They're not puppets, they have minds and wills of their own, and they don't like being bossed anymore than you do. At least, that's the way it is with family horses, ones you've grown up with."

"Yeah, but . . . but Barney *never* obeys unless he feels

like it! Missy wrote to be careful of his mouth, but he won't do anything unless I pull, and she came and saw me *hauling* on his mouth, and I know she won't bring him back."

Mom, thank heaven, took it all seriously. She spent a moment forming her answer. "I'm sure Missy was angry, and you can't blame her, of course. But maybe she'll understand, when she has time to think about it. She's had him long enough to realize how difficult he can be."

"He's probably not like that with her."

"Oh, I bet he is, or would be if she didn't know how to get around him."

"Really?"

"Love, there may be perfectly mannered horses that anticipate your every command and whose only desire is to please you, but I've never met one. And frankly, I don't think I'd want to."

"What d'you mean?"

"If your horse did everything you wanted, all the time, it might as well be in a book, or in your head. The resistance is part of its being real, if you see what I mean." Like the difference between games with toys and games with people, Sarah thought. Unpredictability was part of their being alive. But realizing that didn't help her much now.

"Do you think she'll send him back?"

Mom frowned. "Probably. I understand how she feels,

of course, but she does need a place for him, and that gives you another chance." She stood up. "I'm going downstairs now—come on whenever you're ready."

Slightly comforted, more by being talked to realistically than from any new hope, Sarah lay back listening to Mom's retreating steps. Just before she reached the bottom of the stairs, the phone rang. "For you, Sarah. It's Albert."

Albert's voice sounded childish over the phone. "Hi, Sarah. Happy Thanksgiving."

"Same to you. Did you eat a lot?"

Albert groaned. "I could hardly walk away from the table. Hey, you want to go for a ride and work some of it off?"

Regret and worry made Sarah's voice sharp. "I can't. I don't have a horse."

A pause. "Oh, I forgot. Well, there wouldn't be time to go far anyway. When do you get him back?"

"I don't know."

"Hey, Sarah, are you all right? You sound really strange."

"Yeah, I'm fine. Um . . . I'll come up sometime this weekend, OK?"

"OK, be seeing you then. Bye."

"Bye."

Now she didn't feel like going back upstairs. In the living room, Dad and Gramp were playing chess, and Mom and Gram were talking, mostly about old friends in

Boston. That wasn't too interesting, but they were bound to branch off soon. Sarah sat on the hearth to listen.

Gramp looked over at her, grinning. "So, getting calls from the boys already, are you? Starting early?"

"No." Sarah felt herself blushing. Idiot! Gramp always asked her about the boys; it didn't mean anything. But now, of course, he had a specific boy to ask about.

"Who is this Albert? What's he like?"

That was always a difficult question, even if you'd been friends with someone since second grade, and she really didn't know Albert that well. "Oh, he's very nice," she managed.

"Seems like a good kid," said Dad. "He could stand to lose a few pounds, but he's polite and intelligent, and he shares her mania for horses. Nice boy. . . ."

"Which reminds me," Mom interrupted skillfully, "do you know if Pete and Elaine know where we are?" Sarah shot her a grateful look. Ridiculous to talk about Albert as if he were her boyfriend—and even more ridiculous for her to be embarrassed by it!

The phone rang again. "Will you answer that, Sarah?" Mom asked, from the depths of her chair. Sarah went to the phone. "Hello."

"Hello, Sarah? This is Missy O'Brien."

Sarah's heart leaped wildly. She couldn't get a word out, even if she *had* been able to think of something to say.

"I noticed yesterday you seemed to be having some trouble with the Bear, and I thought maybe if you could come over sometime, I'd give you a few pointers. Would you like to?"

Sarah's voice exploded with relief. *"Yes!* Yes, I'd *love* to!"

Missy laughed. "Tomorrow afternoon OK? Good, I'll see you then. Happy Thanksgiving!"

(11) A Lesson

Sarah stood for a moment before the O'Briens' front door, her heart thumping heavily, before she dared to knock. Mr. O'Brien answered. "Hi, Sarah, come in. Missy's in her room—I'll call her." He led Sarah into the living room, where Mrs. O'Brien sat in her chair, the black cat on her lap. A rocking chair was pulled opposite her, and a half-finished game of checkers sat on the coffee table between them.

"Hello, Sarah. How are you?"

"Fine, thanks. How are you?"

"Oh, very well." Mrs. O'Brien's broad, happy smile was new to Sarah. "Missy tells us you've been having problems with Barney."

Sarah flushed. How had Missy told it? she wondered. "Yes, I have, a little."

"I'm not surprised. He's pretty set in his ways, I guess. Probably should have warned you, but it's been so long since we brought Missy through her growing pains with him that I didn't think of it."

"He gave *Missy* trouble?"

"Endless trouble," said Mrs. O'Brien with a fond smile. "He was . . . oh, Missy, darling, make sure you wear a heavy coat. Dad says it's cold out."

Missy nodded, and crossed over to pat the cat in her mother's lap. Velvet stretched luxuriously, made a whirring sound, and forced her chin over Missy's fingers; while she was occupied scratching the cat, Sarah studied her closely for the first time. Somehow, before, she'd missed the prettiness, the intelligence, the determination in Missy's face. She'd seen only her rival—now she was seeing another person, an interesting one.

"Sorry, Velvet, that's enough," said Missy, moving away from the unsatisfied cat. "Well, let's get going, Sarah." She went into the kitchen, got sugar lumps and a ragged denim coat, and led the way to the barn.

They went in through a small side door, and a dark, cluttered storage area. Somewhere farther on, Barney nickered, a hard, impatient sound. "Coming, Bear," Missy called. He nickered again. They rounded a corner, and there he was, looking eagerly over the stall door. He stretched his nose out to Missy, who grabbed the twitching upper lip. She held it, laughing, while Barney wriggled. He freed himself and nosed her pockets.

"Pig!" She slapped his neck affectionately, making the dust fly. "All you think about is food." Barney swept the sugar cube off her palm. He chomped twice, nodding his head thoughtfully each time, and reached out his nose again, first to Missy and then to Sarah.

"No more till you've done some work," Missy told him firmly. She led him out, tied him in the aisle, and handed Sarah a brush. While Sarah groomed, she picked out his hooves. Sarah watched, fascinated by the ease with which it was accomplished.

"He picks them up when you say 'Foot, please'?"

"Usually; but he never lifts the right front without a fight. You just learn to live with that."

Sarah's brush reached the ticklish spot over the hip. Barney jerked his foot up warningly, and Sarah flinched back as she always did. Then she caught Missy's frown, and flushed.

"Don't do that," said Missy quietly. "Barney *never* kicks, and you must never seem afraid of him. Besides, if you *were* dealing with a kicker, stepping back would be the worst thing to do. You stay close to a kicker; that way, they can't get much of a swing, and the blow is softened."

"Oh." Now that Missy reminded her, Sarah remembered reading that somewhere. She finished brushing Barney's plump quarter, and went up to get his forelock. He decided what he wanted more than that was to rub his head on her shoulder, and did so with his usual vigor, almost knocking her down.

"Cut it out, Bear," said Missy, coming up to catch his halter. "It's my fault he does that, I'm afraid. I used to rub his head after a ride, when he was sweaty under the bridle, and now he thinks it's OK any time." She took the brush and went into the little room beside the stall. Peering in, Sarah saw a warm, glossy grain bin, and the bridle and saddle hung on pegs just like hers. Missy brought the tack out, and settled the saddle on Barney's back.

"I suppose you found out about his bloating?"

Sarah's mind flashed back to the first day, and the ridiculous image of herself sitting on the sideways saddle. "Oh, boy, *did* I!"

"His favorite trick. He even catches me sometimes." With just as much effort as Sarah usually had to put into it, she girthed him up. Then she bridled him, led him outside, and tightened the girth another notch. "I'll just take him around to see how he's going to behave." She swung into the saddle, lightly and gracefully. Sarah saw a subtle change in her face as she settled herself, a combination of contentment, fondness, and firmness.

She spoke to Sarah and they set off at a brisk walk. Sarah angled around to see Missy's hands; light, following hands, the kind *she* had always been praised for. Easy enough at a walk, she thought. Let's see how you do when he wants to get back to the barn.

Barney was trotting now, a long sweep across the field and back. In the middle again, they slowed slightly, to circle at a sitting trot. Sarah was surprised. She hadn't seen a signal, and her admiration rose again. To circle at a trot, *she* always had to pull very obviously. But how did Missy do it?

Barney dropped back to a walk. This time Sarah saw the signal, but it was very slight. And how freely he moved, dropping his nose softly to the bit and slowing in balance! Missy walked him to one end of the field, turned, and lifted him into a canter.

They made a lovely picture, Barney's mane and Missy's hair flying in the wind he made, Missy rocking, supple and close to the saddle. She took him in a large circle back to the center of the field and guided him through a figure eight, with a smooth flying change of leads. At the completion of the last loop she brought him back to the middle and halted, with only one walking step. He stood quietly, though the wild swiveling of his ears betrayed his excitement. Then, the final touch to a beautiful performance—show off, Sarah thought enviously—Missy backed him, six calm steps. She turned him then toward the barn and Sarah. His steps quickened eagerly, but Missy held him to a walk in some soft, unseen way. She halted him beside Sarah, and dismounted.

"He's full of beans today," she said, looking satisfied. "Just as well. I want to see him at his worst with you."

And me at my worst with him! But admiration won out over jealousy. "I couldn't tell he was feeling that way. You made it look so easy."

Missy glanced at her sharply. "Don't let appearances

fool you. You have to work hard to make it look that easy." Sarah's heart sank. Missy seemed suddenly very stern. "Mount up. You'll work in the middle of the field, in a circle around me. Let's go." She started out and Sarah followed, trying to relax tense arms and follow the motion of Barney's head.

Missy stopped. "All right, walk him in a couple of circles around me." But Barney didn't want to move away; Sarah had to pull him. "Use your legs," came Missy's quiet, inflexible voice. "Outside leg behind the girth, inside *at* the girth. Bend him, don't pull."

Legs! Of course! In all her agonizing over her hands, she'd let her legs hang practically idle. Disgusted with herself, Sarah applied leg pressure as she'd been taught long ago, and Barney turned. She put him on a circle around Missy.

"Your form's good," Missy commented after two turns. "Wider circle now, at a sitting trot."

Sitting to Barney's trot was never easy, and Sarah concentrated on relaxing the small of her back and deepening her heels to absorb the jolts. Barney started speeding up, a little more with each circle. At first she did nothing, hoping he'd slow by himself—she didn't want to pull and show Missy how bad she was. Finally, though, his speed made it impossible to sit. Sarah gave a hurried little tug. Barney stuck his nose out and went faster, and Missy shouted, "Whoa!"

Barney stopped dead, and Sarah rocked forward on his neck. Missy stalked out to them, her face smooth and dangerous. "I saw that coming. Sarah, you simply *must* check him, constantly. If you'd just lightly fingered the reins when he first speeded up you'd have been fine. Instead you let it go, and he decided to see how much he could get away with. Now try going the other way, and this time *pay attention!*"

Deeply mortified, Sarah turned around and trotted again. This time Barney tried earlier, one ear cocked back cannily. Sarah fingered the reins, bouncing a step as she forgot to concentrate on her seat. Barney steadied, but almost immediately tried again. She slowed him, and this time he accepted the verdict, at least for a while.

"That's better," Missy called. "You're getting the idea, but you could still be lighter. Remember, he's only as light as you are. If you use a light signal early enough, he'll respond lightly. If you pull, he'll pull. Turn around and work it the other way."

And so it went, for another hour. The moment Sarah relaxed, Barney would try something. Sarah would correct him, and looking at Missy's face, know she'd still been too harsh. She struggled to stay one thought ahead of him, and in the end it seemed to be working, but she couldn't tell. He might just have been tired.

Missy called it quits when Barney started to sweat. "He's even harder than other horses to cool out in the winter, 'cause of all that hair. You want to be careful of that."

Then she *would* be having him in the winter! Missy was going to let him come back to her! Sarah's heart did cartwheels all the way to the barn.

They unsaddled him, blanketed him, and walked him till he was cool. Missy was quiet now, withdrawn. She didn't speak again until they were back in the barn, taking off the blanket.

"Well, Sarah, I think all you need to do is keep your mind more on your riding. Barney isn't the kind of horse you can moon around on. He demands your attention. You'll find he's absolutely trustworthy when you're in trouble"—Sarah remembered the docile horse who'd carried her to the Joneses after her fall—"and if you're not in trouble he'll get you there fast, unless you watch him."

"Can't you *ever* relax with him?" Sarah asked despairingly.

Missy smiled. "Yes, of course. He wouldn't be a good horse if you couldn't. But you have to learn when you can, and when it would be dangerous, and the only way to do that is by observing him." Barney pushed her, impatient with all the talk.

"Yes, Bear, I've got your treat." She gave him a sugar cube. "Sarah has one, too—here, Sarah, he always has a treat after he works. C'mon now, into your stall." She took off the halter and Barney walked in obediently, checked out the feed box and hay rack, and turned back to them. Missy rubbed the wet patch below his ears.

"I don't know if I've explained it very well, but I hope you understand a little better. It won't be easy at first, but it'll be worth it. He's a great little horse."

Sarah thought so, too, and aching to try out what she'd learned, she had a hard time getting through the rest of the week. She read every book she owned, had Jill over to make fudge, trained the hapless Star to stop barking on command—she couldn't be taught not to *start* barking—and went to Albert's for supper, getting her first look at how a dairy farm works. But it was a long time till the Thursday afternoon when Missy brought Barney back.

She rode him over through a light sleet, looking tense and sad and worried. Silently she unsaddled him and turned him into his stall.

"You be good," she said, stroking the little dents above his tricornered eyes. "Mind Sarah, and don't do anything stupid like break a leg."

A horn blew in the yard; Mr. O'Brien had come to drive Missy home. A last, desperate hug for Barney, and she was gone.

Sarah went to Barney's head. He was gazing after Missy, and hardly seemed to notice her. She scratched the itchy spot under his mane. Absently he responded, scrubbing his lip on the top of the half-door, his attention still on the yard. With a sudden fury that frightened her, Sarah slapped his shoulder.

"Darn you, Barney, look at *me!* You're *my* horse now!" He flicked an ear at her. "Maybe you don't think so, but you are! And you'll like me just as much as her. You'll have to, 'cause sometime she's going to decide she likes some guy more than you, and then I'm going to buy you and you'll be *mine!*" Barney lifted his head and neighed toward the yard. Wearily, Sarah turned away.

By the next afternoon it had warmed up, and the glaze of ice melted. Sarah rode; how much better the world looked from horseback! A hard bubble of happiness formed in her chest. She relished the perky bob of his head, the awareness of each foot touching the ground, even the pressure on the reins as he bore toward the barn door, hoping to dash through. Gently, she corrected him before he could even get near. He made sour ears at her. "Sorry, Bear."

Barney kept on testing his luck, but riding him was easier today than it had ever been. Even out in the pasture, where he usually staged a pretty good exhibition of educated disobedience, Sarah felt securely in control. Almost always, she caught him before his naughtiness could get far, and returned him to the straight and narrow without taking drastic measures.

It wasn't until she was unsaddling that she realized why it was so easy today. Today there were no daydreams, no distracting thoughts. After a week on the ground, riding Barney again was all the daydream she needed.

And that was the key to riding. You had to be in it fully, savoring all the details the way you did to make a daydream real. You had to ride for riding's sake, and not for the dreams it carried you to.

"Oh, Barney," she cried, hugging his sturdy neck joyfully. "That's it! I understand—and boy, are you in for some trouble!"

(12) The Hunter

The Sunday after Barney came back, Sarah and Albert planned a long ride. For Vermont, it was being an unusually mild winter, but this might be their last chance to get out before the ground was covered with snow. Jill couldn't go, and Sarah was guilty of feeling a little relieved. They could go much farther if they didn't have to wait for short-legged Ginger.

Once he was sure he was going to see his friends, Barney strode briskly along the road. His ears shifted interestedly, noting every noise and movement. Sarah pulled him well off the road whenever a car passed, and still he danced.

There were a lot of cars, because today was the last day of hunting season. Mom had warned her to be careful, and made her wear a red shirt of Dad's over her jacket. Now, seeing the cars bristling with guns, and the way the men looked out the windows, she was glad she had it. Stories flew around school of the dogs, cows, and people that hunters had mistaken for deer; they'd been careful to keep Star close to the house since the season started.

Mr. Jones was just leaving the barn when she arrived. He waved and called, "How d'you like this weather? S'posed to have gotten three feet of snow last night, but I'm not complaining."

"Me either."

Albert came around the corner leading Herky. Mr. Jones paused on his way to the house. "Where you kids headed?"

"Up the Woodfield Mountain Road. We won't go all the way, though. Too cold."

Mr. Jones frowned for a moment, considering. Then he shrugged. "I guess it's all right, if you stick to the trail. Just be careful. Last day of the season, woods're full of trigger-happy fools ready to shoot at anything to get their deer. And mind the horses don't spook, too." He slapped Herky on the rump. "Go on, then, and watch out."

The road over Woodfield Mountain, once well traveled, had dwindled to a treeless strip through the woods. A carpet of brown leaves rustled under the horses' hooves. Albert took the lead, because he knew where the rocky places were. Not that Herky cared much about the footing; he rolled over all kinds of terrain like an agile tank. Barney had to scramble to keep up, and as usual, this kept him out of mischief so Sarah could think of something else. Ah, what had Missy said: "You have to know when you can, and when it would be dangerous."

Other than the noises of their passing, the woods were oddly silent today. Only the jays were out, their voices unusually raucous as they flitted through the treetops, like bits of fallen sky. Occasionally a shot sounded, far away, and Sarah would say, in the most irritatingly righteous voice she could manage, "I hope *that* deer got away."

Albert had created a small rift in their friendship by getting a deer the first week of the season. While Sarah knew, deep down, that the Joneses could use the meat, and that their brand of hunting was different from the sports hunters', she wouldn't let herself forgive him.

Twisting and drifting to find the easiest slope, the road wound gradually up the mountain. It had been built for a slower, horse-drawn age, so there were places to rest, and a watering trough halfway up. Albert was very enthusiastic about it, and scornful of the modern roads that took the direct, dull route.

Sarah, in an argumentative mood, said, "I thought you'd be all for progress, with all your science fiction. Isn't that what it's all about, making things easy and dull?" Albert made no answer; probably because he couldn't think of one, Sarah smugly surmised.

A lone squirrel scuffled in the leaves beside the road, and Barney lunged forward, crashing into Herky's rump. Herk shifted his hips, threatening to kick, and Sarah and Albert found unity in scolding their mounts. After that, an unspoken truce prevailed.

They were a little more than halfway to the top, with cold hands and noses, each wondering how to suggest turning back without seeming cowardly, when they saw the deer. A young buck, it was feeding in an abandoned orchard beside the trail. Every few seconds it flung its head up, ears twitching, to stare off toward the stone wall that bordered the orchard. Its tail stayed at half-mast, ready to snap up into the white danger signal.

Sarah and Albert pulled up to watch. For a minute or two the deer eyed them suspiciously, but despite its jumpiness, it didn't seem alarmed. It turned its attention again to the woods beyond the wall. Its nervous glances became longer in duration. Once it trotted off a few steps, head and tail high, but circled back to the tidbit it had left. It only looked their way if one of the horses stirred.

With a shriek, a jay rocketed out of a tree beyond the wall. The deer froze; only one ear twitched, like an independent thing. Then it took a small, jerky step, lifting its knees high. Another—the still air exploded with the gunshot.

Barney leaped almost out from under her. Sarah's mind caught at tags of sensation; his odd little grunt, hauling on the reins, dancing white deer tail bounding away—branches slashed her face—ouch, one in the eye—tears—"Whoa, Barney! Whoa!"

Barney stopped on his own, circling around to crash against Herky. Albert never even noticed the squashing of his leg. He was screaming after a red-clad, running figure beyond the stonewall. "Goddam you, come back here, you goddamed idiot! You come back here!" Sarah was astonished to see tears on his face.

As Barney pressed closer to Herk, she said, "The deer got away, and we're OK. Don't get hysterical, Albert." She made her voice as scornful as possible, hoping to get his attention. He turned, his mouth squared like that of a child crying.

"You don't understand—it's Barney! He hit Barney!"

"No," said Sarah faintly, her mind refusing to grasp it.

"Yes, he did. I saw blood fly!" Albert was already wrenching his leg from between the horses and dismounting. Sarah sat shaking her head, too dazed to follow. Then Albert groaned. The sound released Sarah from her frozen sickness, and she tumbled out of the saddle.

Albert, his face old and weary, was staring at Barney's chest. Cringing, Sarah looked. Her eyes flinched away, carrying only an impression of red wetness. She gazed desperately at the ground, at the blood dripping on the brown leaves.

"How bad is it?"

"I don't know. Darn it . . . we've got to stop the bleeding." He threw his jacket on the ground, tore off his flannel shirt and undershirt, and packed them against the wound, covering it. Sarah could look again. "There. Maybe it's not so bad. I don't think the bullet went in, but I don't know. If we can just get the bleeding stopped— But I don't see how we'll move him, even then."

"Bert, one of us has to go get your father."

"Oh, right. You go, you shouldn't stay here alone."

"No." She could barely speak past her chattering teeth. "Please . . . Barney, I can't leave Barney. He . . . just *go!* You know the road." She pressed her hand beside his on the shirts. "Hurry!"

"Right." Albert thumped her shoulder reassuringly, and struggled back into his jacket. He vaulted onto Herky. "Half an hour," he shouted, reined around, and thundered out of sight.

That half hour seemed to last days. Barney was frightened. He twisted his head, crying for Herky, and each time he did, Sarah felt the tightening of muscles around the wound and imagined a rush of blood. He shifted nervously on his hocks—his front feet were rooted, as though he didn't dare move them—and was startled by the rustle of his own hooves in the leaves. Sarah's one hand pressed Albert's shirts to his chest, and the other clutched his bridle. She couldn't pat him, or scratch him, or do anything soothing.

Well, I could talk, she realized hazily. Her tongue stuck to the roof of her mouth, and when she got it going it felt thick. "OK, Barney, it's OK. They'll be back. Herky'll be back, poor Bear, and Albert will bring Mr. Jones, and he'll get you all better. Steady—I don't think you're bleeding as much, but if you don't hold still you'll start again." On and on, chatter that she didn't think could possibly be calming; she sounded nervous even to herself. At first, head high and ears pinned back, Barney paid no attention. Then one ear came questingly forward, flicked back, swiveled forward again to listen. He lowered his head till his muzzle rested on her shoulder; she could feel teeth. It was a position he sometimes took when she was doing something he didn't like, a reminder that he could be dangerous if pushed too far. Now, it only meant that he needed comfort.

A dozen false alarms disappointed her: the wind, a squirrel, a blue jay, or something unknown, far away. At last, though, she heard the steady, grinding whine of a truck approaching.

As it came closer, Barney became worried, tossing his head fretfully. But the truck stopped out of sight, before it could get close enough to really scare him. A pounding, rustling noise of feet heralded Albert's arrival. He was red-faced, and too out of breath to say anything. Mr. Jones followed more slowly.

"Whoa, Barney." He held out a leathery hand for Barney to sniff, and bent down to look. Cautiously, he peeled the shirts away. A thin line of blood started to trickle, but the main flow had stopped. "Looks like you were right, Bert. A glancing tear—the bullet didn't lodge. But he'll need stitching. Mother's calling the vet, going to have him meet us at your place." For the first time he looked at Sarah, with sharp, kind eyes. "All right, young 'un?"

Sarah nodded, patting Barney's neck with her free hand. There was a small stain of blood on the palm that she didn't want to look at.

The walk down to the truck was the longest of Sarah's life. When they finally got Barney going, he moved in short, stumbling steps, shaking and snorting. Going downhill must have been torture for him, with all his weight thrust on the chest muscles. At one point, when they'd rested him for five minutes and he was still blowing and rolling his eyes, Sarah thought they'd never get him down. But at last the truck came into view.

Herky was inside, looking huge and cozy in a red plaid blanket. He let out a great, bellowing neigh when he caught sight of his friend, and Barney's nostrils fluttered in reply. "We brought him to keep Barney calm," said Albert, looking anxiously at the big chestnut. "Hope he doesn't get chilled—he was pretty hot. . . ." Sarah felt a stab of worry. Herky couldn't be hurt, too. . . .

Barney paused a long time at the end of the ramp, pawing loosely in the air with his right leg. He seemed afraid to step up the necessary two inches. Only desire to get to Herky finally conquered his reluctance. Albert and Mr. Jones linked hands behind him and helped him up the slope.

When he was wedged in securely, they blanketed him, and rigged a bulky, makeshift bandage. "We'll see," said Mr. Jones, looking sceptical. They got into the cab and began the rough ride down the mountain. At each bump, the sound of scrambling hooves tore at Sarah's heart. She kept seeing Barney down, bleeding, trampled. Mr. Jones drove grimly on, trying to get the ordeal over as quickly as possible. On the other side of her, Albert sniffled, and she heard his teeth chatter. He'd ridden off with his jacket unzipped and nothing underneath.

"Oh, Bert, I *hope* you don't get a cold," Sarah wailed, breaking a long silence. Albert looked startled and said nothing, but in a moment his shoulder shoved comfortingly against hers.

When they reached the main road they stopped to check. Barney was still on his feet, but the bandage had slipped and the wound was bleeding again. Mr. Jones packed it, and drove swiftly to Sarah's house.

Mom and Dad were waiting in the yard, grim and worried, and together they persuaded Barney to come out of the truck. He would move only after Herky had been unloaded. Then they eased him, step by step, into the barn and his stall, bedded deep in sawdust. Turned loose, he looked to see if Herky was near. Then his head dropped, and he stood by the door, motionless.

"Heard from the vet?" asked Mr. Jones.

"Your wife said he was out when she called, but they'll send him to us right away."

Mr. Jones peeked under the bandage, and pressed it back quickly. "It *better* be right away."

(13) Dr. Raymond

The vet arrived twenty minutes later, a large, red-faced man smelling of cows and antiseptic. "Hi, I'm Doc Raymond. Sorry I took so long." He came into the stall with Sarah and Barney, and pulled away the latest bandage. "Whew! That's a mess. Too bad, he's a darned good little horse. My daughter's ridden against him in shows. Remember me, Barney? I'm the guy who sticks needles in you every once in a while . . . and you're going to get some more today, poor fellow."

He turned to everybody clustered around the stall door. "Could you get me a bucket of warm water, and maybe a drop cord? Light's kind of poor in here." While Mom and Dad were gone, he swabbed a place on Barney's neck with alcohol and gave him a shot. "General antibiotic. Hmm, better go with a tetanus, too.

God, I hate this time of year!" His broad, genial face hardened. "I have more animals come in shot by hunters . . . I know you hunt, Art," to Mr. Jones, "and I don't mean all hunters—but God, the *fools* they let into the woods with a gun!"

Dad came back with a steaming pail of water, and Dr. Raymond splashed a pungent liquid into it. Then he brought out a huge, gleaming stainless steel syringe, filled it with water, and gently squirted it over the wound, washing it. Now that the first shock was over, Sarah found that she was able to watch. The small seepage of blood turned pink, and washed thinly down Barney's chest.

"There." Dr. Raymond put the syringe back in the pail, and patted the wound dry with gauze. This worried Barney a little, but Sarah's fingers, gently rubbing the base of his ears, reassured him.

Mom finally brought the drop cord, and the dark stall was flooded with yellow light. Dr. Raymond now injected a local anesthetic into Barney's chest, and threaded a needle. Mom turned abruptly away, and even Dad looked a little distressed. Sarah stood stroking Barney's neck and watching, fascinated, as Dr. Raymond began putting together the puzzle of torn skin and flesh. It took a long time, and the very center of the wound could not be closed. As Sarah watched, the world narrowed to the haze of yellow light, Barney's marred chest, and the vet's sure hands. Nothing else had ever existed, or would exist.

"There," said Dr. Raymond, straightening finally, blinking his eyes hard. "Want to hand me that bottle of sulfonamide dressing, Art?" He puffed the yellow powder on the open patch. "There, that'll help with the formulation of new tissue." He washed his hands and began putting things away.

Now that the stitching was done, Mom came back to the stall door. She asked the question Sarah didn't dare to. "How do things look?"

Dr. Raymond closed his bag and stood up, stiffly. "It's early to tell. If all goes right, he could heal perfectly. If he gets infected, or feverish . . . well, anything could happen." He turned to Sarah.

"Keep him on bran mashes for the first three or four days, that and a little hay—oh, and *plenty* of water, warm, so he doesn't get colic. And he'll need exercise, too, or the muscles will heal short and he'll be permanently lame. Start late tomorrow, maybe five minutes of walking, and gradually work up from there. That's very important.

"Now, I'll leave a bottle of wound dressing, and some of this antiseptic. Wash the wound twice a day, dry it, and then puff this dressing all over it. That's about all; I'll drop by sometime tomorrow and see how he's doing." He rubbed Barney's nose gently with his knuckles, and refastened the blanket. "There, old horse. We'll get you feeling better in no time. It's probably a good idea to keep him covered for a while, and I'll give you a collar so he can't bite out his stitches." He picked up his bag and left the stall, looking at his watch. "Darn, I'm due in surgery five minutes ago."

Mom went with him, and brought back the collar. It was made of smooth, rounded sticks, held together by leather straps, and would keep him from bending his neck. It looked dreadfully uncomfortable.

"Do you think he needs it on tonight?" she asked, as Mr. Jones started to adjust it. "He probably won't feel up to chewing himself."

"Leave it on, or Doc'll have all that stitching to do over in the morning. You folks got any bran?"

"No," said Mom, "I'm afraid we don't."

"I'll send Mother over with a sack. C'mon, Bert, get your nag in the truck. It's getting on to chore time." It didn't seem possible that that much time had passed, but when Sarah looked at Mom's watch, it was almost four.

Albert untied Herky and started to lead him outside. But as soon as he moved away, Barney came to life. With a high-pitched neigh, he turned to lean against the door, staring anxiously after his friend.

"Bring him back," Sarah shrieked. "Barney's pressing his chest on the door!" Hurriedly, Albert turned Herky around and let Barney sniff him. Reassured, Barney drooped again.

"Looks like you'll have to leave him," said Mr. Jones. "Well, get him settled, then." Now that the crisis was over, he seemed fidgety.

"OK." Albert tied Herky beside the stall, adjusted his

blanket, and got him a bale of hay from the mow. He paused awkwardly beside Sarah. "Sorry I have to run off like this. I'd like to stay and help. . . ."

"You better go get warmed up," Sarah said dully. "You'll catch a cold."

"Oh, thanks." Looking very embarrassed, he squeezed her shoulder. "Well, take care, OK? I'd better go, or Dad'll get jumpy." He reached over the door to scratch Barney's ear. "Hope you feel better, Barney. And you be good, Herk. I'll see you all tomorrow."

Warmed by his concern, Sarah watched him out of sight. Thank heaven for good, fat old Albert—and the next time Danny Trevor called him Fat Albert, she'd punch him in the nose! She turned back to Barney.

The first thing was to get him some warm water. She got a pail, filled it at the sink, and trudged back, slopping the water into her boot. Barney wasn't interested. She splashed in it with one hand, to let him know what it was. He paid no attention, and when she took her hand out the cold turned it numb and she had to tuck it quickly into her armpit.

At last, Barney turned listlessly toward the water, flipped the surface with his bottom lip, and then sucked down the whole pailful. Finally, response! Best not to give him too much all at once, though. She took Herky out to the water tub before bringing Barney another pail, which he drained.

By that time Mrs. Jones had arrived with the bran. Mom and Sarah mixed up the hot mash, a very messy process. Dad thought it smelled wonderful, but Barney mouthed it dully and ate only half. At last, Sarah gave up trying to coax him and went back into the house, moving in a fog of exhaustion.

To her surprise, she was hungry. Cold air and hard work had sharpened her appetite. She ate slowly and methodically, her head propped on one hand, trying to think of nothing but the food. At last, though, she was stuffed, and there was nothing else to do. "Guess I'll call Mrs. O'Brien and get Missy's number."

"Good girl," said Mom.

Mrs. O'Brien was horrified. At first she could only ask, over and over, "But will he be OK?" When she calmed down, she refused to even consider letting Sarah call Missy. "I'll call her myself. Such a shock—you're a good girl, but a mother can handle this better. I *will* give her your number, so she can talk to you afterward."

More waiting. Twenty minutes passed, while Sarah dozed uneasily in the big chair by the fireplace. When the phone finally did ring, she jumped nearly out of her skin.

"Hello, Sarah?" A terrible tension in the voice. "Mom said . . . how is he?"

Sarah had to clear her throat. "Well, it looks awful, but the vet says with good luck and care he should heal fine."

"Whew! I was so scared." Missy's voice went shaky with relief. "When Mom said he'd been shot . . . how did it happen?"

Sarah explained as well as she could. The whole thing was still fragmented in her mind. She couldn't understand how the hunter could have missed the deer, that close, or how he could have fired in the first place, when he *must* have seen her and Albert right behind the deer.

"How does he feel?" Missy asked finally, in a tiny, dreading voice.

Sarah had to say, "Pretty bad. But he drank, Missy, and he ate half his bran mash. The vet's coming again tomorrow. . . ."

"Doctor Raymond?"

"Yes."

"Thank God. He's wonderful."

"Yes, and Mom and Mr. Jones—he's a farmer up the road—will tell me what to do. I'll take good care of him, Missy."

"I know. It's just . . . darn, why did I have to go to school so far away? If I could only come *see* him, and help . . . darn!" She'd been feeding in coins as the operator demanded them, but, "I'm out of money. I'll call tomorrow, OK?" Sarah's reply was cut off.

She hung up and went out to the kitchen. "I'm going to take another pail of water to Barney and go to bed."

"I'll do that for you," said Dad. "You're too tired."

"No, I'll get it."

She was surprised to find it snowing out, fat, puffy, endless flakes drifting through the flashlight beam. Already there was a coating on the path deep enough to make tracks in. It seemed years since morning, when she'd rejoiced that the snow hadn't come.

Herky nickered sleepily as she came in. He'd finished his hay and was standing close to Barney's door. Sarah fondled his big head a moment before daring to look into the stall.

Barney was still in the same place, his ears back in a strained expression. He looked at her with brief interest, then dismissed her, ignoring the water. The wound hadn't changed since she'd last looked. If only it doesn't get infected, she thought. But there was nothing more she could do tonight. She left the water beside him and went back inside. There she ran a deep tubful of warm water, got in, and, half an hour later, Mom was tucking Sarah in bed. "You've done well today, dear," she said. "We're very proud of you." Giving her a quick, tight hug, she left. Sarah fell asleep immediately.

(14) The Gift

The sky was still dusky when she got up the next morning. Dressing quickly, she ran a pail of warm water and hurried out to the barn. She was greeted with a nicker from Herky and, wonder of wonders, a high-pitched little neigh from Barney. He was looking cautiously over the stall door, not daring to raise his head high because of the stiffness, but very eager. He almost knocked her over to get to the water.

Hugely relieved, Sarah went back inside to make the bran mash. Barney still wasn't very hungry, though, and kept looking back hopefully at the empty water pail. Sarah got him some more, letting Herky finish the mash.

Now she had to wash the wound. She tied him up short and began gingerly, wincing every time he did.

When Dr. Raymond had done this, he'd had a syringe, and the wound was fresh. Now it was crusted with dressing, and Sarah had to work with wet, chilled fingers.

Finally, though, the wound was clean, and she puffed dressing over it. Then she watered Herky, got more water for Barney, and hayed them. Barney wanted his hay enough to stumble across the stall for it. Sarah's heart soared. She never thought she'd ever get so much satisfaction out of a horse's greed. She picked out his stall and put down fresh sawdust, and just when she was pausing to lean on the stall door and feel self-approving, Mom called.

"Sarah, breakfast."

"Oops, see you two this afternoon." She ran to the house, kicking in the knee-deep, fluffy snow. Under a clear, brilliant sky, the yard sparkled like a Christmas card. Star, delighted, was bouncing through the drifts and rolling ecstatically on her back, inviting Sarah to play. "Sorry, baby, no time." She gulped her breakfast, and hurried down to the bus stop.

At school, she and Albert were overnight celebrities. Everyone crowded around them, clamoring for details. Sarah was furious at their macabre interest: they didn't care about Barney at all! Or her and Albert, for that matter. Fortunately, Jill was there. Sarah lost herself in the flow of chatter and pretended not to hear anyone else.

Today was the day she was finally supposed to go to

Jill's house. Jill had always put it off, but last week she'd finally said yes. "'Cause the boys have basketball and Marie's got a party, so there'll only be two kids at home instead of seven." Now Sarah couldn't go. Jill's bright string of chatter broke for a minute when she realized this, and a fleeting look of disappointment crossed her face.

"Maybe I can come Saturday," she said, and Jill nodded, though she still didn't look happy.

School blurred by, and she jumped off the bus, to hurry up the crunchy, snow-packed road. She heard Star barking from the bottom of the hill, and when she came into the yard, there was Dr. Raymond's pickup. She rushed in to find him in the stall, examining Barney.

"How is he?"

"Oh, hullo. Much better; no fever, and the wound looks good and clean. You've done a good job." He glanced at his watch, and his eyebrows jumped. "By George, I've got fifteen whole minutes before I have to be anywhere! Good, let's see if we can get him walking."

While Sarah got Barney's rope, Dr. Raymond led Herky away from the door, and stood holding him by the opposite wall. Sarah liked the picture they made to-gether, the big red horse and the large man with the weatherbeaten red face.

She haltered Barney and led him out. He shuffled on his front feet, tossing his nose impatiently, doubtless annoyed with the collar as well as with his injury. Sarah let him hobble across to rub noses with Herky.

"He's good and stiff," said Dr. Raymond. "Just lead him up and down here for me a few times."

"Just leading" Barney was more difficult than it sounded, since he didn't particularly want to move. Sarah had to speak very sternly and keep flicking his ribs with the rope end. Dr. Raymond leaned against Herky, talking to him and watching. At last he nodded.

"Good enough. Make sure he gets that twice a day, starting tomorrow. By next week you should be able to take him outside when it's not too slippery, but wait till I come again before you do that. And now I *do* have to go. I'll be seeing you."

While she was helping Barney back into his stall, Albert arrived leading Ginger. His voice sounded croaky, but otherwise he seemed well.

"Hi, how is he?"

"Better." Sarah told him all about Dr. Raymond's visit, and he looked satisfied. Then he got Herky's bridle out of the tack room.

"Hi, Herk, you big lunkhead. Yes, I'm taking you home, but you gotta leave your pal Ginger here." Ginger had already shouldered her way to Herky's hay pile.

"Thanks for doing this, Albert. He really *does* need a companion right now."

"Get him and Star used to each other."

"Hah! I'd like to keep my baby dog all in one piece, thanks." Chasing Star was one of Barney's favorite occupations when healthy.

"You could get him a goat, like they do for nervous race horses."

"That's a wonderful idea! I *love* goats." But her mind quickly skipped back to the newspaper ads. "They cost fifty or sixty dollars, though. Mom just barely got a job, and we're still living on macaroni and cheese. I couldn't."

"That's too . . ." Suddenly, Albert's eyes sparkled, and his mouth curved in a smile that usually meant he'd moved one of your checkers while your back was turned, and was waiting to see if you'd notice. Catching her eye, he ducked his head, and when he came up the smile was gone. He bridled Herky, and Sarah gave him a leg up.

As he was leaving, he paused to say, "Y'know, Sarah, you really should get up to Jill's Saturday if you can. She doesn't invite people much—it's kind of important, I think."

"That's what I thought. I'll make sure to go."

"All right. Bye, I'll see you tomorrow."

The week settled into a new, far busier routine. Sarah got up early to make Barney's breakfast, to clean and dress the wound, to lead him up and down the front of the barn for a few minutes, and to water him and Ginger. Then, after school, the whole process was repeated.

The wound began showing a little healthy pink in the unstitched patch, and it didn't bleed anymore. Barney's mood improved, too. He was grouchy about exercise, and nipped if he felt she was pushing too hard, but at rest he seemed his old self again. Each evening Sarah wrote a report to Missy, and on Friday a big package of carrots arrived in the mail. Sarah took one out to Barney.

"Missy sent these—she didn't come herself, though. Wonder why not. *I* would. Maybe she's found someone to be in love with. But don't worry, Bear, I want you even if she doesn't." She walked back to the house, her head filled with graceful speeches of thanks for the gift of the unwanted Barney.

Saturday morning, after chores, Dad drove her over to Jill's house. It was low, long, and rectangular, like the look-alike boxes in the suburbs, but messier and painted dark red. Two hounds were chained to doghouses in the yard, and around the corner was a chicken run and a large shed. Jill introduced her all around; first the hounds, Moses and Sam, and then the chickens, pecking in their snowy yard and lifting their yellow feet high. They all had names, and each belonged to a certain brother or sister. After the first few Sarah lost track, because Jill kept correcting herself until the matter was hopelessly confused. Finally even she gave up, and led Sarah into the warm, pungent goat shed.

They were greeted with a chorus of bleats; Sarah was amazed at the range of expression, from stark indignation to imperious command to piteous weakness to joy and surprise and "Well, it's about time!" Jill snapped on a light and Sarah stared, dumbfounded, at a sea of long, elegant ears and roman noses.

Actually, there were only six goats in the first pen, all reaching out their noses eagerly. Jill got a measure of grain to divide among them, and while she fed them she told their names: Aunt Marion, the matron, Frankincense, Myrrh, Tawney (short for Milligatawney), Faline, and Bingo.

"How come you have so many?"

"Oh, these are only the milking ones. You haven't seen the yearlings and kids and William—he's the buck—yet." Jill was leading her through another door. "See, Ma needed goat's milk to feed Brian, 'cause his digestion was bad and he was always sick, so she got Aunt Marion, and *she* had Frankincense and Myrrh next Christmas. She just kept breeding them, and she sells the milk to the health-food store in town and gets money enough to buy our winter clothes every year, and for eight kids that's a lot. . . ."

Slim, graceful yearlings stretched out white-freckled, black and gold noses, begging for handouts. And in the next pen over, miniature goats with immense, floppy ears jumped at the walls, trying to see over.

"Hi, babies. Yes, we're coming in." They climbed into the pen and squatted down, and all the kids gathered around them, sniffing, sucking fingers, and chewing clothes. Sarah picked up the littlest, a tiny golden thing with freckled ears longer than its neck. It was amazingly soft, and looked very wise and pious; its amber eyes always seemed to be turned toward heaven as it nibbled

Sarah's buttons, ears, and nose.

"She's beautiful," Sarah exclaimed, enchanted.

"Yes, isn't she? We're trying to get Mom to keep her, we all love her so much, and she's so . . ."

Sarah interrupted ruthlessly, as she had long since learned was necessary. "She's *so* sweet, aren't you, little Goldy?" The kid tasted Sarah's chin with a soft little tongue. "Oh, Jill, I *wish* I could buy her. Barney needs a friend while he's sick, and Ginger can't stay forever . . . what are you laughing at?"

Jill pushed a kid off her lap and stood up. "They tickle! Come on inside, it's almost time for lunch and we're having . . ."

Inside, Sarah began to understand why Jill talked so much and never listened. The rooms were dimly lit, cluttered, crowded, and filled with noise. The television blared in the living room, someone was playing records in a downstairs bedroom, and a radio was going upstairs. Loud voices shouted over the din: "Who stole my sweater—" "It's *your* turn to set the table—" "If you touch my model, I'll tell Ma—" Jill's father frowned at his football game, occasionally bellowing at them all to shut up, and her mother clattered in the kitchen, trying to get dinner around the children and seven cats. In this house nobody could hear if they were talking too much, and nobody listened. It must be like being deaf, Sarah thought, when you talk too loud or too soft because you can't hear yourself. They all seemed cheerful enough, but you'd have to be to survive. She understood now why Jill was always eager to come to her big, sparsely populated house.

After lunch, they went sliding. "But first we have to give the babies a little grain." How eagerly the little noses plunged into the trough! Sarah got in again to pat Goldy's back, as she shoved amongst them with small, sturdy shoulders. Every time Sarah touched her, the tiny, white-tipped tail would waggle. Sarah could have stayed all afternoon watching her, but Jill called her impatiently to go sliding. They had a glorious time on the long hill behind the barn, but on the way back, cold and wet, Sarah had to stop to see the kids again.

Goldy was asleep when they came in, her nose tucked into her flank and one ear covering her back almost completely. Her little tail twitched, and she made sucking noises, as if dreaming. Sarah bent to touch her, and in the deep, trustful sleep of youth, Goldy didn't stir. Suddenly, Sarah was consumed with longing.

"How much would it cost to buy her?"

"We get about sixty dollars for a doe kid," said Jill offhandedly. "Stop mooning over her and come inside. I'm freezing."

It was almost time for Mom to pick her up anyway. Sarah sat close to the wood stove, nursing her hot chocolate and thinking of Goldy. She wanted her, in the way she'd wanted things as a little girl, so fiercely it almost hurt. Well, this was impossible, though. Maybe when she was grown-up she could raise goats. . . .

"Your mom's here."

Jill walked out with her to say good-bye. Just as she reached the car she gasped, "Oh, no, can you wait a minute, Mrs. Miles? I forgot Sarah's Christmas present—I'll be right back . . ." and she dashed away. Sarah got into the front seat.

"Oh, Mom, you should see the baby goats! They're *so* beautiful and soft and sweet, and there's one . . ." The words, pent up in a long afternoon of not being listened to, gushed out, and she was still chattering when the back door opened. She turned automatically to see the size of the package, and sagged against the seat, dumbfounded. The package was one very small, golden goat, wrapped in an old red sweater.

"Merry Christmas a little early," said Mom quietly.

"What?"

"Your father and Albert and Jill and I went in on her together. I know it's early, but we thought you might need her before Christmas. You won't mind not getting very much else, will you?"

"It was Alb's idea," said Jill proudly.

"Oh!" Suddenly Sarah understood the meaning of things that had been bothering her all week—mysterious conferences between Albert and Jill, unexplained phone calls to her parents, the fragments of a discussion she'd overheard. Everything fell miraculously into place. But all she could do was murmur "Thank you," which seemed hopelessly inadequate, climb over into the back, and take her goat onto her lap.

(15) Christmas

Goldy conquered everybody's heart without any difficulty. Mom and Dad were instantly charmed, Star went sappily maternal on sight, and even the sceptical Barney was soon won.

At first he sniffed her over very thoroughly, jerked his nose in disapproval, and curled his lip. Then he ignored her for a while, as if hoping she'd go away. Unaffected, Goldy explored the stall contentedly, quite happy, until Sarah left her alone. Then, bleats of amazing volume pierced the quiet of the barn, bleats of panic, loneliness, apprehension, mounting to a crescendo of anguish. Alarmed, Sarah went back to peek, being careful not to let Goldy see her.

The kid, like a child in a temper tantrum, stood absolutely still, neck outstretched, shrieking. Barney, intrigued, stumbled closer, and touched her with his nose.

As if by magic, the bleats stopped. Goldy turned wonderingly, her upturned eyes worshipful. Barney's nose swirled over her back. She gave a tiny murmur and moved close to him. Sarah left them, satisfied.

From then on, Goldy was *his* goat, to be jealously guarded from the yearning Star and all people. Goldy, of course, had her own ideas. She loved her big friend, and liked to stay with him, stealing his food, sleeping curled among his legs, and following him at exercise. But she liked playing with Star, too, and going into the house for treats and to bounce on the couch cushions when Mom wasn't looking. Poor Barney was often left to neigh after her. In a while she would come trotting back, ears flapping to her rolling sailor's gait, or cutting wicked capers. Her antics made exercise more fun for them all, and since there was now a half hour of walking morning and night, entertainment was welcome.

Time flew by, crammed with work and play and Christmas secrets. And then Sarah came home on the last day of school to find Missy in Barney's stall. She was standing with one arm thrown over his withers and her free hand rubbing the base of his ear, talking to him in a low, loving murmur. When she noticed Sarah she broke off, looking embarrassed.

"Hi, Missy."

"Hi, Sarah." She gave Barney's withers a hug and Barney followed, moving his upper lip on her shoulder in his customary demand for attention. He barely seemed to notice Sarah. "I got in late last night," Missy was saying, "and I've been bothering my poor Bear since about noon."

As Sarah just stood there, not saying anything, Missy shifted uneasily. "Um, that wound looks *awful!* What does Dr. Raymond say about it?"

Somehow, Sarah got her voice started again. "He's pleased with it. If you can wait, he promised to drop by today."

"Oh, I'll certainly wait."

"Well . . . um . . . excuse me, I have to change." She made her escape, running across the yard to the house. Inside, she thumped her books down on the table and burst open Dad's door.

Dad was just sitting there, staring blankly out the window. Goldy lay beside his chair, knees primly folded, nibbling at a bowl of Rice Krispies. She looked up and gave a contented little "meh" of greeting. Dad turned.

"Hi, Peanut. What can I do for you?"

"Nothing. I just want Goldy." She scooped the little goat up in her arms and carried her upstairs. That was against the rules, but right now Sarah didn't care. In her room, she set Goldy down on the floor, flopped beside her, and cried onto her thick, soft coat.

After a moment or two of this, Goldy squirmed free and wandered over to taste the book bindings. Sarah watched blurrily.

At last, she said to the white-tipped, waggling tail,

"He loves *her* best, he always will. He never even *looked* at me." At the sound of her voice Goldy came back, standing up on Sarah's knee to nibble her ear. Sarah took the kid onto her lap, and leaned back against the bed. She stroked Goldy's plush coat slowly.

"At least *you're* mine, baby. Nobody can take *you* away." Oh, but it was so awful. Lately, she'd almost forgotten that Barney belonged to somebody else. He'd seemed so much her own . . . oh, she felt so tired. She could sit there all afternoon, softly stroking Goldy.

But Star and the crunch of tires announced the arrival of Dr. Raymond. Reluctantly, Sarah changed and went downstairs, Goldy clattering behind her.

When she got out to the barn, Dr. Raymond was talking to Missy. "I know it looks pretty bad, but it's healing just the way it should, thanks to Sarah. She's done a terrific job of dressing it and exercising him, and generally keeping him fit. You'll have her to thank for a sound horse in the spring." Yes, *you'll* have a sound horse, Sarah thought, but Dr. Raymond's approval took away some of the hurt.

"Well, I do thank you," said Missy softly, her hands still fondling Barney's head.

Dr. Raymond went into the stall for a closer look. "It's healing pretty darned well," he pronounced. "Keep up the good work—or are you taking over now, Missy?"

Sarah tensed. Missy gave her a quick, sidelong glance. "I don't think I could," she said. "He'll be staying here, of course, and besides . . ."

"Doctors are never asked to treat family members," said Dr. Raymond, with an approving smile. "I nursed my wife's cat through a bad injury, and never again. Too harrowing." He stood taking the three of them in for a moment, seeming to see and sympathize with the tensions between them. "A wise decision—he couldn't have a better nurse. Merry Christmas, all." With a pat for Goldy, he was gone.

Sarah bent to pat Goldy, too, hiding her face. Missy's doing this so I won't feel bad, she realized, and didn't know whether to be thankful or resent it.

"I hope you don't mind being drafted," said Missy tentatively.

"You don't *have* to, you know." She was ashamed of her ungraciousness, in the face of Missy's poise, but she was only tenuously in control of herself.

"I suppose not," said Missy, "but I'd rather. It'd be very hard for me to start tending him—I couldn't stand to hurt him."

Sarah nodded. She could understand, and it was good to be truly necessary, but just now she couldn't be very happy about it. With a muttered "Thanks," she went back to the house, leaving Missy and Barney together.

Christmas came, full of presents despite Mom's warning. Gram and Gramp sent a pair of riding gloves and three horse books; Mom's parents sent a collar and bell for Goldy, a homemade nightgown, and more books.

Christmas afternoon they had a party for Barney. Mr. O'Brien and Missy, Jill and Albert and their parents,

Mom and Dad and Sarah, all gathered in front of his stall, to drink steaming hot chocolate out of Thermoses and watch him munch his carrots. He seemed to enjoy the company, and he loved having his picture taken, posing prettily every time someone aimed a camera.

Everybody made much of him, but Sarah and Missy took care to visit him separately. Luckily, there were enough people so their discomfort with each other didn't upset the party. Only Albert seemed to notice, and he understood without having to be told.

Missy was home for two and a half weeks, and visited Barney almost every day; Sarah always waited till she was gone before going out to do the chores. Then she returned to college, and life resumed its casual smoothness. Underneath, somewhere, Sarah carried the ache of a lost dream; beyond all doubt, Barney would never be hers. But spring was far away, and for now she could ignore it.

In February Dad typed the last period in the first draft of his manuscript, sent the swivel-chair whizzing across the room, and took a two-week vacation. He chopped wood, repaired the house and barn, and cooked dinner every night, looking more relaxed and satisfied than Sarah had ever seen him. Within a few days, though, he was repeating to himself at regular intervals how *very* rested he felt, and two weeks to the day after he'd left it, he plunged back into the writing room and closed the door. After that, he emerged for a few hours a day to tell them what agony rewriting was, and that was all they saw of him.

The snow vanished for a while late in March, and Barney, with a complex pink scar on his chest, was turned loose in the barnyard on sunny afternoons. He always exploded out of the door, bucking and squealing, to start a vicious-looking game of chase with Goldy. The little goat fled him, but when he halted she returned to square off and butt at his nose, her ears flying at wild angles. Barney would jerk his nose out of range, and nip her rump, and she would bleat furiously. Poor anxious Star yelped from the other side of the fence.

One warm Saturday, when the water was gurgling and rushing down the slope of the pasture, Dr. Raymond dropped by. Sarah caught Barney and held him still while he was examined. He was full of spring devilment, and kept resting his muzzle on Dr. Raymond's backside with a suspiciously innocent expression. "Watch it there, you ungrateful little brute," the vet rumbled. "Turn him loose."

Sarah unsnapped Barney's rope, and he charged across the barnyard after Star, who'd ventured in to talk to Goldy. "Not a hitch," said Dr. Raymond. "I'd say you could start riding him lightly, Sarah. Take it easy on hills and make sure the footing's good, so he doesn't slip and pull those muscles. And if he stays sound, go ahead and work him as normal."

"Oh, *thank* you!" Ever since the start of warm weather, she'd been aching to start riding again.

Barney and Goldy wandered over to them. Dr. Raymond reached under Barney's mane to scratch his neck, rubbing off a shower of loose winter hair. Barney's upper lip squirmed with pleasure. His scratching reflex prompted, he dropped his nose to Goldy's rump and began swirling. Goldy curved her body in itchy response, looking thankfully heavenward. Dr. Raymond laughed.

"That, Sarah, is one of the greatest joys of having animals—just seeing them be themselves. Never mind all the undying devotion stuff you read in the romantic books. Mostly that's dreamed up in the writer's head. You either get affection from animals, or you get tolerantly ignored." He paused, consideringly. "It seems to me you have animals for the feeling *you* have for *them*, not the other way around. It's a wonderfully undemanding kind of love."

Somehow, the idea sounded right; Sarah wasn't quite ready to accept it yet, though. Storing the words away for future consideration, she went inside to call and see if Albert wanted to go riding.

Barney was elated at the prospect of going somewhere. Neck arched, ears pricked, he bore on the bit and Sarah pulled back before she remembered that long-ago lesson. "A quick check and release—no, firmer—ah, there!" She brought him back to a prancy, reluctant walk. He tossed his head, trying to get the reins away from her, and only bumped against her firm hands. Frustrated, he snorted loudly. His scimitar ears swiveled as he investigated the roadside, looking for something to shy at. Sarah rejoiced in his high spirits and his springy, lively, *sound* stride. Her attention was undivided, and despite the sense of being aboard a capricious bundle of dynamite that might choose at any moment to explode, she felt firmly in control.

As they neared Jones Dairy, his eagerness grew. At the sight of the big red barn, he neighed. A high squeal from Ginger and a rumble from Herky answered. Now there was no holding him to a walk. He barreled into the yard, loudly proclaiming his own arrival and shouting out all the winter's news. He was feeling better and Missy had been to see him, and he had this new friend, a goat. . . .

Albert leaned out of his upstairs window. "Hi, Sarah. Hey, he looks great! Hold on, I'll be right down."

In a moment he was there, flushed and coatless. With a sudden shock of recognition, Sarah realized how much weight he'd lost over the winter. For the first time his shoulders looked broader than his stomach, and you could see the bone structure of his face. Sarah was forced to admit that he was good looking. Not like David Harrison at school, that everybody was in love with, but he definitely had his good points. . . .

"What're you staring at, Sarah?" She started guiltily.

"Boy, he looks happy to be out. Lemme bring the guys to see him." He went behind the barn, and in a moment Herk and Ginger trotted out. Sniffing, pricking of ears, and occasional nips and squeals went into the reunion, until Sarah began to feel uneasy above all this plunging horseflesh.

Albert rescued her, getting halters and tying up his horses. Sarah dismounted awkwardly. Already, her legs felt molded around Barney's barrel, like those of the cowboy who rode her model horses.

"You'll be stiff as a board tomorrow morning," said Albert cheerily. "C'mon, tie him up and help me groom."

Jill arrived a few minutes later, tumbling out of the car at full steam. She'd gotten up late, and there were new kittens, and Aunt Marion had had twins this morning, that was why she was late. Albert and Sarah exchanged smiles over Ginger's back.

"Well, where do you want to go?" Albert asked, when the horses were tacked up. "Bemis's trail ought to be pretty well open by now."

Sarah thought with longing of the quiet wooded trail, twisty, hilly, and adventurous. It was one of her favor-ites—and it wasn't *very* long. It probably couldn't hurt . . . no. Much though she wanted to go, she couldn't make it feel right inside.

"I'd better not. His Majesty shouldn't tackle anything like that for a while."

"Oh, I forgot. Tell you what, then; we'll ride home

with you over the logging trail. That's not too hilly, and we can go somewhere else after, if these fatsos aren't too tired."

"Thanks," said Sarah, and they mounted and started off, talking happily, the horses bouncy, eager, and competing for the lead. Sarah felt a warm, hard bubble of joy expanding in her chest. This was what she wanted; this was the best and only way to live.

(16) On Woodfield Mountain

A little bit of snow fell after that, but not enough to hamper their riding for long. In the next few weeks they rode almost every day. They explored again all the trails they'd explored in the fall, and found new ones. Once they got lost for almost an hour, and Albert was late for chores. The girls tried to help him make up for lost time, but only managed to get in his way. They rode in sunshine so hot that the horses came home sweaty, in spite of being walked the last mile, and in cold, raw winds, and once in the rain. For the first time, Sarah smelled the warm, pungent aroma of a wet horse working. It was a little like damp feathers and a little like ordinary dry horse, but combined, the scents made something magically new, and unforgettable.

Barney was shedding in good earnest now, and Sarah

came in from every trip to the barn coated with rich bay hairs. Goldy, too, was losing her woolly undercoat, and left bits on the corners of the couch, where she insisted on rubbing whenever she came inside. The poor couch had received so much abuse since they'd moved that Mom was abandoning her attachment to it, and when Goldy came trotting purposefully in, she only looked resigned.

The happy spring wore swiftly on. Despite the lengthening days, and the extra hour of riding gleaned from daylight saving, time slipped through Sarah's fingers. Missy wrote to say she'd be home May twentieth; Sarah didn't count the days, hoping that they'd pass slower that way, but one Friday morning she woke up and realized that the twentieth was only a weekend away.

In school, even Jill noticed her glumness, and she came up with a dozen schemes for kidnapping Barney, for proving to Missy that he loved Sarah best, even for raising money enough to buy him. Sarah couldn't plot with her. There just didn't seem to be any point.

More constructively, Albert brought up the long-deferred plan to ride over Woodfield Mountain, and they decided to go on Saturday.

Sarah's alarm woke her at six, and she padded downstairs to get ready. She liked being alone in the yellow light of the kitchen while it was still dusky outside, making breakfast. For the first time, she managed to flip her egg without breaking the yolk. Then, to pack a lunch. She invented a roast beef, tomato, lettuce,

and cream cheese sandwich that promised to be deli-
cious, providing that it survived the trip. A few green
olives in a sandwich bag, two apples to share with
Barney, and a Thermos of milk completed the picnic.
She stowed it all in her knapsack and took it to the barn.

She caught Barney, brushed him, and tacked up.
Next came the far more difficult task of capturing
Goldy. She had to be shut in or she'd follow them, but by
now she knew exactly what was going to happen, and
she wasn't going to allow it without a struggle. She
wandered here and there, nibbling casually at new
shoots of grass with one eye cocked warily in Sarah's
direction. Just when Sarah's hand snaked toward her
collar, she trotted on a few steps farther. Finally Sarah
gave up pretense and chased her openly. Goldy loved
this. Every time Sarah lunged, she charged out of reach,
ears flapping, tail straight up, and bell tinkling wildly.
She ran with the grace of a small steeplechaser, but
Sarah was far from admiring her. At last she got a pan of
grain; Goldy was always conquerable by greed, and was
soon locked in Barney's stall, bleating plaintively.

Sarah stuffed Barney's halter and rope into the knapsack—that couldn't be doing her fragile sandwich much
good—and shrugged it onto her back. As she mounted,
she had a sudden vision of herself at riding school: a
self-confident girl, properly attired, riding a well-man-
nered Thoroughbred around the ring to gather blue
ribbons in the school show. How horrified her instructors would be to see her now, in jeans and a flannel

shirt, with a knapsack, setting off on self-willed little Barney and not at all sure who was going to be in control today. "You're a good Bear," she told him hopefully. "Let's go."

They arrived at Jones Dairy just as chores were getting finished. Albert was spreading a fresh layer of sawdust; Sarah helped, and by the time they were done Jill had arrived. They caught Ginger and Herky, groomed and saddled them, got Albert's lunch, and they were ready to go.

As Sarah mounted, she heard the crackle of paper in her shirt pocket; oh, yes, the envelope! She took it out and handed it to Albert. "Here, Dad sent this. I almost forgot."

At first she thought he wasn't going to open it, but after staring at it a moment, he tore open the flap. Sarah strained to see, without seeming too obvious. Dad wouldn't tell her anything last night. "Sorry, Peanut, if Albert wants you to know, he'll tell you."

Albert was reading one of the pages inside, his face slowly getting redder and redder. Finally he looked up, and seeing their eyes on him, tried to seem casual. "Just a story Sarah's father read for me," he said airily, and tossed it on a shelf in the barn as though it didn't matter. But Sarah knew it did, and from the look on Albert's face, she thought that Dad had probably mixed his criticism with quite a bit of praise.

The last time they'd been up Woodfield Mountain, the trail had been deep in leaves. But the leaves had been pressed under the snow all winter, and now, wet and shining, they covered the ground smoothly. The horses' hooves cut through to the dark earth underneath. The smell here was different than in the fields—cooler, faintly spicy. The trees were just beginning to leaf out, making a bright, lacy canopy overhead. Small birds tumbled and squabbled in the treetops, where before there had been only jays. The jays were still there, floating on their wings of fallen sky, but their voices were less raucous.

They passed the little orchard. There was the place where they'd stopped last fall, there the deer had foraged, there by the stone wall the hunter had risen up and fired. This all had to be explained to Jill. When she understood where they were, she actually stopped talking for a moment. Sarah watched Barney carefully, but he didn't seem to remember the place. God, how long ago it all was!

From here on, the trail was new to her. It twisted up steeply as they neared the top; in places it was only a jagged bed of stones, where the spring rains had washed it. The horses scrambled over these places, Jill usually dismounting to make it easier for Ginger. Agile Barney managed splendidly; Sarah gave him his head and abandoned herself to the enjoyment of his power, knowing that while he had to concentrate on the footing he couldn't be naughty. Herky rolled on, unflappable.

"Are you still going on the Hundred Mile Trail Ride this fall, Bert?"

"Yup. I earned the entry money this winter, and there's all summer to get him in shape." A pause. "Y'know, Sarah, you could help me condition him, since you won't be having Barney." Sarah's heart sank, remembering. She forced herself to listen.

"I'll have haying and stuff to do, so maybe we could work out something where I'll work him in the morning and then pick you up at your house. You could bring me home and take him back to your place, work him in the afternoon and keep him overnight. Then you could bring him over for his morning work—or something like that."

"Poor Herky," said Jill. "Sounds like he'll be going all day."

"He needs it. He's a big boy—lots of fat to get rid of. Would you like to, Sarah?"

"If it would really help . . ." It did sound like a good idea. Lots of running around, but at least she'd be able to ride, and she'd be helping Albert to maybe win the trail ride. And there'd be a horse around at least part of the time, to fill the barn and keep Goldy company. Wish it was going to be you, though, she thought, patting Barney's neck.

Hunger pangs overpowered them at the top of the mountain, though it was only quarter to eleven. They compromised by eating half their lunches there, and saving the other half for when they got to Woodfield. The ground didn't seem wet till you'd been sitting awhile, but when they got up they all had wet pants.

"It'll help us stick to the saddle," Jill said, but in the meantime it only made mounting difficult, as their wet pants clung to their skin.

They were heading downhill now; the wet leaves made the trail slippery, and Barney fretted, tossing his head and trying to go off at angles. Sarah thwarted him most of the time, but once in a while he surged off through the brush, and she had to fight him back onto the trail.

Behind them, Jill started to sing "The Bear Went over the Mountain," stopping in the middle to explain how appropriate it was, considering Barney's nickname and where they were. Then all three of them took it up, singing as loudly as they could. They went through it three times, and repeated snatches at intervals.

At the bottom, they decided to finish lunch in the Woodfield village square. That would give plenty of opportunity to impress whoever was interested with their long trek. They felt like mountain men, coming down from their wooded haunts to rough up the town; slouching in their saddles, they played the role as they'd learned it in books and on television. This was only among themselves, of course. An old lady who knew Albert's mother stopped to talk, and Albert spoke to her as one civilized. Jill and Sarah, behind him, tried to make their faces tough and truculent, and ended up giggling helplessly.

They stayed until a man came out of the general store with a shovel, and said for them to clean up all the droppings before they left. Deciding that civilization was a foppish thing, for foolishly scorning their gift of high-grade fertilizer, they cleaned it up and returned to their mountain fastness.

On the way back up, Sarah could feel Barney straining under her. His neck hair was rough with sweat, and he was obviously tired, but he gamely held his position in the lead, refusing to take second place to Herky. They hurried as fast as the tired horses could safely go, but Albert was still late for milking. Sarah and Jill offered to help, but he said he could work faster without them, thanks.

Sarah rode slowly home, alone. Even the prospect of seeing Goldy and having supper couldn't hurry Barney now. Sarah was tired, too, and her hips and ankles ached. She kicked her feet out of the stirrups and let them dangle; amazing how good a simple thing like that could feel. Barney stretched his neck out on a loose rein, his ears flopping at weary angles. Getting him tired is one way of making him behave, Sarah realized.

"Poor Bear, we're almost . . . home." Two days left.

(17) Prospects

Missy was coming for Barney on Monday afternoon, so Sunday was their last day together. Sarah had half expected Albert to call, but he didn't. That was OK; she wanted to be alone today. She rode up the logging trail behind their barn, with Goldy and Star tagging along.

Star wandered far off in the woods, as usual, and Goldy stuck close, complaining. Barney insisted on stopping regularly to sniff her over from nose to tail and think about her. Despite her gloom, Sarah couldn't help laughing at this obvious ruse. "Faker!" Oh no, said Barney's ears. He was truly concerned.

They came to a fallen tree, too big to jump, and she turned him aside. He plowed through the brush with Goldy, outraged, at his heels. On the other side, Sarah suddenly realized that it would never occur to her to be on guard against his trickery there, though the opportunity was perfect. With her arms up to protect her face, she couldn't have stopped him.

Missy had said you had to know when you could trust him and when you couldn't, and she'd spent a long time trying to feel that out. Now, though, it came instinctively.

So, she decided half regretfully, it didn't mean that she'd won. It only meant that she knew the rules. There were times and places for each of them to be in control, just as there were times and places for continued testing. The horse-book authors and riding instructors might call that nonsense, but Missy would probably agree.

Goldy was lagging farther and farther behind, and her complaints sounded genuinely desperate. Looking back, Sarah realized that the fat little goat was exhausted. "We'll have to cut our ride short, Bear." He didn't mind, but she did. This was probably the last time they'd ever set off into the woods together. Reluctantly, she turned him around. He stopped to nose Goldy. What is she going to do without him? Sarah wondered. Poor Goldy, losing her best friend.

Back at the barn, she unsaddled and cooled him out, lingering over the routine. This was the last night she'd measure out his grain into the black rubber pail, the last time she'd rub Vaseline into the scar while he munched. She bent to look at it; a faint fuzz was starting to form on the pink railroad tracks. He'd have hair there soon, but she wouldn't see it.

When he was through with his dinner, she opened the gate and watched the two of them head downhill, Barney snatching mouthfuls of grass and Goldy ambling beside him, challenging him to head fights.

She took the pail and Vaseline back to the tack room and stood there for a moment, looking at the polished saddle and bridle on their pegs, the brushes, the fly-repellent, the box of medicines, all neatly arranged. She tried to fix everything in her mind, so she could never forget it. Then, drearily, she squatted down and began packing the smaller things into the pail. Mom was taking them over in the car tomorrow afternoon, and Missy was riding Barney home; Sarah didn't want to have to face packing after he was gone.

That night, she couldn't concentrate on homework. The words and numbers whirled through her head and vanished out the back. When Mom and Dad came up, she was sitting at the desk with her head down on her math book.

"Sarah?"

She started and looked toward the door, pasting on a smile. "Yeah?"

"Just checking. Haven't heard a peep out of you all evening." They came inside, and Sarah turned backward in her chair to face them, bracing herself. It would be talk about Barney, wise counsel about loving enough to let go, about building her character—the last thing she wanted. Dad was obviously the one who was supposed to start, and the silence stretched on while he tried to formulate his beginning. Sarah couldn't read Mom's expression.

At last Dad looked away from the picture of Barney, and launched into speech. "Sarah, there's . . . there's one thing I didn't really think about when I said yes in the fall, and that's how attached you'd become to . . . Barney." The hesitation was natural to Dad. He couldn't really think of horses as having names, the way people or dogs or pet goats did. "Maybe if I had, I'd have said no, I don't know. You put an awful lot into him to have to give him up."

"At least now she's got him to remember," said Mom quietly. It was right, but not comforting. Sarah's face stiffened into a mask to hold back her hurt.

"Well," said Dad, clearing his throat, "that's as may be. Sarah, I realize the last thing you want is a lot of talk right now, but you should know that I've changed my mind. Your mother'll be teaching full-time next year, the book is almost finished, and money isn't as tight anymore. And I no longer have any doubts about your accepting the responsibility. So we've decided to afford you a horse, as soon as we can, and you'll love the new horse, too, when you get to know it."

In spite of herself, Sarah felt a tickle of excitement. "You're really sure, Dad?"

Mom laughed. "He's worried sick that Goldy's going to be lonely."

"And yes, I approve on your account, too," said Dad. "Now, I'm afraid you'll still have to survive a horseless summer. We'll do our buying in the fall, when your mother tells me the prices are down, and I hope by then we'll have the advance on the book. That OK?"

"Oh, Dad! And Albert's going to let me help condition Herky, so I'll be able to ride. But . . ." Unexpectedly, her voice choked off, and her eyes filled with tears.

"Look, it's almost ten," Mom said briskly. "Why don't you give up on the math and go say good night to him? Oh, and I'm letting you stay home tomorrow, in case Missy comes early. Do you want to?"

"Yes, I think so."

The last good night. She sat at the desk for a few minutes more after they left, trying to think. Her own horse—what would it be like? She couldn't imagine anything but a short-legged, furry little half-Morgan. Well, she'd try to buy a half-Morgan, if there was one to be had. But it wouldn't be Barney. It wouldn't have pink, fading scars on its chest, that she and Dr. Raymond had healed from a gaping wound. It wouldn't have the same doe-eyed naughtiness, or even like to be scratched in the same spots.

On the other hand, it would be *hers,* to know, to love, to train, to keep. She wouldn't always know it loved someone else best, or have to keep in mind how someone else wanted it handled. And she *would* love it as much as Barney, someday, when she knew it as well.

Well, life went on. She got up from the books, went

downstairs to get a coat, and went out. Barney would be in the barnyard; he always came back at about this time.

When Sarah came out, Goldy rose, with a small, sleepy grunt, from her resting place on the front step. She stretched, shook herself, and walked along with Sarah, her bell tinkling quietly. The moon was almost full, making it easy to see the path. A soft breeze blew on Sarah's face. Her boots squelched pleasantly in the mud.

Barney stood dozing in the far corner of the yard, his lip sagging till his teeth showed. He started at Sarah's call, and looked around sleepily, his ears expressing mild curiosity. Unusual to have visitors this late. After considering for a moment or two, he turned lazily and ambled over. Lifting his muzzle to Sarah's face, he blew his warm, sweet-smelling breath on her. He stayed that way a moment, then, with a sigh, began nosing her pockets.

"Sorry, Barney-Bear. Nothing." She rubbed his neck under the heavy mane. His hair was mostly shed out now, though his belly and hindquarters still looked shaggy. He nuzzled energetically at her shoulder, telling her he'd like a scratch, please. She scratched. So did he, tickling her with his whiskers. She had to keep reminding him not to nip, that she wasn't another horse with a lot of cushioning hair. Goldy slipped through the wire and rubbed herself against his legs, grunting ecstatically.

The front door opened, casting a yellow rectangle of

light across the yard, and closed again. In a moment
Star trotted down the path, sniffing out Sarah's trail
with an eagerly wagging tail. She didn't dare come too
near Barney, so she sat a few feet away, looking wistful.

At last, Sarah began to get cold. She stepped back.
"Well, g'night, Bear." She couldn't feel as sad as she
wanted to. She'd pictured herself coming out here to cry
brokenheartedly all night, but now she only felt a vague
melancholy, and the new, rushing excitement of knowing she could have a horse of her own.

"Sorry, Barney. I do love you." She came back, put her
arms around his nose, and kissed him. Barney flattened
his ears and tossed his head, pretending to hate the fuss.
But when she stepped away, his ears snapped forward,
and he stretched out his muzzle. Sarah stroked it,
velvet-soft and whiskery. "'Night, Bear." Star jumped
up, mouth open in a panting laugh. Sarah tugged one of
her silky ears, and they went back to the house together.

Since she didn't have to go to school, nobody woke her
the next morning. She came down to find Mom gone,
and Dad busy typing. She fixed an egg and some toast,
fed Star the crusts, and went out to bring Barney up
from the pasture. She might as well have him ready
when Missy came.

Of course, he'd rolled in the night, and he was filthy.
Sarah unpacked the curry comb and a brush and
cleaned him up. By the time he was gleaming, *she* was
filthy. She went inside to wash up, and when she came
out, Missy was there.

She was standing close to Barney, talking to him, and she seemed surprised to see Sarah. "Hi, I didn't think anybody was home."

"Yeah . . . I stayed home to see him off. . . ." Her voice trailed away, and an awkward silence fell. Neither of them could think of what next to say. Sarah finally remembered something. "Um . . . Mom'll bring the stuff over later this afternoon."

"OK."

There really wasn't anything else that needed telling, though the silence seemed to demand something. Sarah turned to stroke Barney's nose, and Missy patted his neck. In a moment she said, "The wound healed beautifully. Thank you."

"You're welcome." Sarah cleared her throat. "See, the little hairs are coming in already, and if you rub Vaseline on every day he might not even have a scar."

"You think so?" Missy bent to look again. Sarah absently began to scratch Barney's neck, and he scrubbed his lip on Missy's back, where her shirt had come up.

"Hey, you brat!" She twisted out of reach. "Sarah, I'm really grateful for the care you've given him, and . . . well, I'm sorry I have to take him away from you, 'cause I know you love him, too."

Sarah hadn't expected anything like this. Her eyes filled, and she looked away. "Yeah, I—I will miss him. But I'll be getting a horse of my own in the fall." She said it as much to cheer up Missy, who was looking regretful, as to remind herself.

"Really? That's wonderful!" Missy came completely alive, all awkwardness gone. "That's great! Hey, I'll keep an eye out for anything that looks like what you want. What *do* you want?"

"Something as much like Barney as possible—ouch!" She rubbed her hip. "But with better manners and *no teeth!* Ow! He hasn't done that in months."

"A parting gift. Barney, you beast. Just for that, you're getting saddled."

Sarah watched, feeling slightly satisfied that Missy had to struggle with the girth, too. She bridled, slung the halter over her shoulder, and mounted. Once mounted, she seemed on the verge of leaving, but reluctantly. When she spoke, it was slowly, each word carefully considered as it came out. "You know what, Sarah—why don't you come over one day a week this summer and I'll give you a lesson on the monster? Who's been in control most lately?"

"I—I don't know," Sarah stammered. "We switch off, I guess."

"Well, I can make sure you're on top more often, give you a little dressage training—do you jump?"

"A little."

"I'll teach you—oh!" Missy squealed suddenly, like Jill in a wilder mood. "Wonderful! I can't ride in junior horse shows any more, but *you* could. Would you like to?"

"Yes," Sarah gasped.

"Great! Oh, this'll be so good for both of you, and it'll be an excuse for me to go to shows, too. . . ." Missy was flushed with excitement.

Barney caught some of it and began to fidget. "He wants to go," said Missy, looking eager herself. "'Bye, Sarah, I'll call you soon, OK? Thanks again."

Barney checked Sarah's pockets once more, hopefully. Then Missy touched him with her heels, and he set out.

Before he'd gone two steps, Goldy bounced around the barn into his path. Sarah ran to collar her, while he nuzzled her back absentmindedly. "Have to stay, Goldy," Sarah told her. They watched their friend down the driveway. His neck arched proudly, and his short, springy stride seemed to bounce with happiness. His tail swished joyfully.

Goldy cried after him. "Sorry, baby," Sarah said. "You can come to my riding lessons and see him, and Herky'll be here part of the time." She swallowed to get rid of the stiffness in her throat. "And in the fall . . ."

"Sarah, telephone." She turned to see Dad's red, abstracted face disappear from the doorway. When she got to the kitchen, Goldy at her heels, the typewriter was already clacking furiously.

"Hello?"

"Hi, Sarah, this is Jill. You didn't come to school today and Alb and me were worried, so we decided we'd call at lunch and see if you're OK. Are you? Is he gone? Is Goldy OK? Sarah, are you really all right?"

A miraculous pause—no, Jill was actually waiting for an answer! "Yes, he's gone." Sarah cleared the huskiness out of her voice. "And I'm OK. Jill, guess what? My parents told me last night that I can get my own horse in the fall."

"*What*? Alb, she's getting a horse in the fall! Get a dapple gray jumper like His Lordship in that book we read last week. . . ."

Albert's voice now—he must have pried the receiver away from Jill, and he was shouting over her chatter, "Get a trail horse and go on the Hundred Mile with me next year."

Jill had the phone again. "Or a huge black stallion, Sarah, you lucky duck! You'll have a perfect black stallion, faster than the wind, and only you can ride him, and . . ."

Sarah broke in. "No, I'd rather have a horse like Barney, that doesn't care who rides him as long as he gets his own way." Jill rattled on, unhearing, but Sarah didn't listen. In a corner of her mind, she was building another dream horse, a small, shaggy bay with an innocent face and an independent soul.

". . . wild and noble and perfectly obedient with you. . . ."